The Curse Chronicles
Spellbound
Book I

By
Maggie Kirk

Table of Contents

"Deep into that darkness peering, long I stood there wondering, fearing, doubting, dreaming dreams no mortal ever dared to dream before"

~Edgar Allen Poe

The Raven

Chapter 1

Sicily 1645

Damien was relieved when the gathering ended. It had gone longer then he had expected it too. He was sure that Esmeralda was exhausted with everything she had just gone through and he wondered how she was going to fair with the long journey home. It was a huge turning point for his daughter. He looked at her as they walked through the thick woods and wondered what she was feeling after finding out what her father was, what she had become.

He looked at the blank, tired face of his beloved daughter and wondered if she thought of him differently then before their trip. He had prayed not. He didn't think he could bare having her look at him with anger, disappointment, or with questioning eyes. He desperately wanted to ask but for the first time in his life he was a bit afraid and couldn't find the right words. He instead kept his eyes on her as they fought the thick forest; sadden to know that from this moment on, his little girl would be forever changed.

They walked in silence for some time

before Esmeralda spoke. "Father, when did you know that I had your gift?" She asked as she suddenly sat down on the truck of a fallen tree.

Damien stopped, wishing to have this talk when they were in one of the safe places along the way or better yet, when they arrived at home. He knew they needed to make it back before Hollow's Eve, but he wanted her to feel that things between them were going to be no different. So he took a seat next to her on the mossy tree trunk and took her hand into his.

"Do you feel that?" he asked as he brought her hand up to his chest and held it tight over his heart. She let out a little gasp and pulled her hand away.

"What was that?" She stared surprisingly.

"That my dear is our special connection that only ones with our gifts can feel. I knew it the moment your mother laid you on my chest when you were a baby."

"Is mother like us?" She questioned.

"No. That's why she isn't with us. She wasn't invited."

She shot a glare at him, "I wish she was here."

"Me too. We can talk more, if you like, once we settle for the day, but right now we need to keep moving," he said seeing that night fall was upon them. The others at the gathering explained to Damien that it was safer to travel during the day and to lay low at night.

"Why must we hide at night?" she questioned as she looked around the creepy darkening woods.

"Your way too young to have to know all this at once but I suppose you must," he decided to tell her a little at a time hoping to not overwhelm her. It was a lot for him to take in when he found out and as he got older and met Katarina, he knew that there would be a possibility that any child they had, could get the gift too. "You see, there are people out there that want to hurt people like us."

Esmeralda's usually bright eyes darkened with fear, "What people? Why father?"

"Essie, you, me and the ones at the gathering are different then other people, like your mother," he tried to explain but his words weren't coming out as smooth as he wanted.

"Mom wants to hurt us?" she asked riddled with panic.

"No Essie. Not her. She loves us very much. She has known of my gifts for a very long time. She actually had me bring you to the gathering because you were starting to show the signs and we wouldn't be able to cover them up for much longer and we wanted you to understand what you were, the right way, by going to the gathering instead of being confused and scared." He quickly explained to ease her worry.

"Ok," she whispered looking down at the log, picking the moss off of it. Damien could see that she was worried so he put his arm around her pulling her in close to him causing a warm glowing feeling around them. She looked up at him and smile. There was that connection he spoke of.

He smiled back. "Ok Essie, we really need to get going. A small village is upon us and I would like for us to be passed it before nightfall."

"Bad people there?" she questioned looking in the direction they were going before she had sat down.

"I'm afraid so," he said as he watched the innocence leaving his daughter. *What have I done*, he fretted as they hugged and then started on their way again.

They hadn't come down from Italy this way but the others at the gathering said the thick woods would be a safer way then the open roads they had used. He agreed. Going through the woods now, he understood why they were safer. The forest had been untouched by humans.

There weren't any pathways. Damien and Esmeralda had to stop after so many steps to listen to their unfamiliar surroundings. He was grateful for his beloved white owl. He was Damien's eyes in the sky and had helped them along their journey to see what they were coming up on but the thick woods made getting a view harder.

Soon they could hear animals and people and Damien knew they were on the outer edge of the village the others called Messina.

"Shhuussshhh," Damien whispered as he held a finger to his mouth, taking slow cautious steps. Esmeralda clung to the back of Damien's cloak. He knew not only was she getting scared but that the cave they could seek shelter in was right pass the village. He let out a noise to call for his owl to come to him.

The owl landed on Damien's forearm, "What is it my friend?" he asked petting the owl, looking directly into the owls eyes. He saw what the owl had seen. "You did well my friend." Satisfied with the owl's job, Damien pulled out a little treat from his pocket and fed it to him. Damien then lowered the owl so that Esmeralda could pet him before he took to the skies once again.

"Father I'm tired. Can we stop now?" Esmeralda whined dragging her feet through the mossy dirt.

"Soon Essie, we are almost there," he replied. He grabbed her hand and led her a little deeper into the woods. The further away from the village the better, and by the time they got around the village night had come. His owl had taken its' place on Damien's shoulder.

"According to the others, we should be able to find the cave in a few more steps," Damien said looking around. Esmeralda tugged on the cloak.

"Father, is that it?" Esmeralda asked pointing off to the side of them. Damien followed her gaze. There was a dark opening in the side of a hill that was partially covered by dead gnarly branches.

"I think it might be," he said relieved. He too had grown tired.

Damien carefully guided Esmeralda through the mangled mess while owl stayed outside perched on one of the branches.

"Father I'm scared. It's so dark," She whispered clinging to Damien.

"It's ok. It wont be dark for long Essie," he insisted leading her back far enough in the cave that if someone were to go by they wouldn't see any light.

He took a small velvet pouch from his vest pocket and as he threw the powder on the ground, he pulled Esmeralda close to him to shield her eyes from the blast of light that was about to happen. Bam! Crack! And in a quick second the cave lit up, "Ok Essie you can look now."

She turned around to see a small fire burning on the ground, "father how did you do that?" her eyes wide with amazement.

He smiled, hoping it was a sign that she wasn't uncomfortable with him. "One of the many perks to our gift. I'll teach you some of them when we are back at home." He gently rubbed her cheek, suddenly feeling like a heel for doubting how she felt towards him. They both saw the power of their bond. She reached around his waist and hugged him as tight as she could. "I saw a couple of things I need for a few spells and I need to get a few branches for the fire. You stay put. Do not leave the cave," he ordered, "Owl will be right outside."

"Father, can't I go with you? Its scary here." she pleaded looking around.

"I want you to stay here and be warm. I won't be long. Do not leave this cave Essie," he said sternly.

"Yes sir," she pouted.

He hated to see her upset but he needed to go. He kissed the top of her head and took off his cloak and wrapped it around her, "I'll be back in a few minutes. I won't be long, promise." He held her face in his hands and looked deep into her saddened eyes.

"Ok," she huffed still pouting. Damien let out a sigh and left the cave. He instructed for the owl to stay.

Esmeralda was upset that her father had left her in the creepy cave with a fire that was about to go out. It had seemed a long time had passed and she was growing antsy. She knew her father would get upset with her but decided to go out against his order to see if she could find a few branches to put on the dying fire. She took the cloak off and headed out.

She found only a few twigs beyond the cave entrance and started walking further out to find more. Before she realized it, she had gone deeper in the woods then she thought and could no longer see the cave. She began to panic and started running in the way she had come, or at least she had thought.

Damien was ecstatic to find the things he did in the woods that he couldn't find in Italy. Crucial items. He also found a few good chunks of wood and was relieved to reach the opening of the cave. His owl's greeting seemed off.

"What is it my friend?" he asked as he motioned for the owl to move to his arm. The owl obliged. Damien didn't like what he saw through the owl's eyes. *Esmeralda!* He gasped and ran into the cave to see the fire out, his cloak on the ground and his daughter nowhere to be found.

"Essie! Essie!" he called out over and over as he ran out of the cave. He didn't hear her, he didn't hear anything. He put his cloak on and with the owl perched on his shoulder he set out as fast as he could to find Esmeralda before someone or something else did.

"Essie!" he yelled again and again. No response back. He was growing frantic.

He stopped and closed his eyes. He could channel himself to her, to find her location, but he wasn't sure how well it was going to work with him being so upset. He had to calm down to focus unfortunately he didn't get the chance too. He heard a blood curling scream and started running towards it as he dodged low branches and downed trees. *Esmeralda!* He stopped. He was in such a panic that he hadn't realized owl had dug his claws into his shoulders in an attempt to stay on. A low fog was creeping across the ground and if he hadn't just came through the way he was running he wouldn't have known a drop was coming upon him. He stopped suddenly and ducked behind a tree at the top of the hill. He could hear men's voices yelling and females crying.

Damien slowly peered around from behind the tree to see at least ten men holding an assortment of weapons. They were celebrating by raising the weapons in the air and yelling. Damien quickly did a once over of the area and then he saw her. His little girl was being held by one of the men and three other men were holding the women. He didn't remember seeing the women at the gathering and wondered where they came from. *Maybe from the village*, he thought. It was rumored at the gathering that a witch coven lived in Messina and that they had come from Italy to escape the black magic that had swept over their small village.

If they bring harm to my daughter, they will all pay, Damien vowed silently as he tried to think of what to do. He blamed himself, the gathering should have ended a couple of days ago and instead of sticking to the plan, he decided to stay, thinking it might be good for Esmeralda. Had he stuck to the plan, they would have at least been in the northern part of Sicily, if not in Italy by now. He knew the southern end of the woods were not good for their kind with the witch hunts going on and the north end of the woods sheltered the witches who practiced black magic. *If something happens to Essie it will be my fault*, he hissed. His mind was all over the place.

He had Owl perch itself on a branch, "watch over us and if something happens, you go home," he instructed as he stroked the back of the owl, "you have been the best guardian I could have ever asked for." The owl made a sound back to let Damien know that it understood.

With that, Damien nodded and then walked away. He had to get closer to Esmeralda. He walked in the perimeter of the men, keeping his cloak tightly around him, to keep himself from being seen. The women were clearly scared. Damien knew that just beyond the men, on the other side, were the rest of the coven that belonged to the three women. He wondered what they were planning. He knew that there wasn't much he could do. He had nothing prepared. He frantically checked all his pockets and pulled out the pouch from earlier. Not much left. He never thought he would be so helpless.

He watched in horror as one of the men lit up the torch he was holding and another placed one of the women on a stump and hung a rope from the branches above her. She was trying to cast a spell but it clearly wasn't working. He knew from experience that ones of their natures had to be calm and minds clear of chatter. Damien kept his eyes on his daughter and the man that held her.

All of a sudden the lit torch exploded causing the man to drop it catching his arm on fire. The men holding weapons went to his aid and the men holding the women let go of them in shock. It caused just enough of a disturbance that Damien was able to grab Esmeralda and hide her inside his cloak. They moved quickly back up the hill towards owl. Damien caught an eye of the coven that had been captured. They were a few paces ahead of him and he was sure owl would hide higher in the trees. Damien was aware that some witches would steal other witch's guardians. He was hoping that these were not those witches. Damien stopped quickly covering Esmeralda's mouth. He waited a moment and then started moving again.

"Father, why did you do that?" Esmeralda scowled. Damien could feel how scared she was.

"The other witches were sensing that they were being followed. I had no choice. Sorry," he grumbled.

"Are they bad ones?" she whispered.

"I don't know. I don't think so, but I can't be sure," he whispered back.

They reached the top of the hill and Damien called out a signal for Owl and within a heartbeat Owl was perched once again on Damien's shoulder and without stopping Damien guided, "we need to stop long enough at the cave to grab our things. We will have to find a different spot further north. It's not safe here anymore."

"But I'm so tired father," Esmeralda cried.

"I know but we must keep moving," he said sternly.

They found the cave again, owl stayed outside as Damien and Esmeralda ran in. Damien grabbed their packs and quickly doubled back. They were once again on the move. Damien could hear noises from behind them and looked back to see five floating flames closing in.

"Come on Essie. You must run faster," he

demanded, pushing her along in front of him.

Esmeralda was trying but the thick brush and branches made running a difficult task. Damien picked up his pace so much that Esmeralda couldn't keep up and tripped over a tree root, sticking up out of the ground, causing her to fall and Damien tripped over her falling in front of her. She got up to run to Damien, when he heard a gun shot.

"Get down Essie!" he yelled out, but it was too late. She stopped dead in her tracks and just stared at Damien for a moment before her little body collapsed in front of him.

"ESSIE!" he cried out as he scrambled on the ground to get to her. He could hear a man yell 'I got one' and the others cheering. Damien quickly covered her with his body and put the hood up; covering both of them in the cloak making them disappear into the scenery.

Damien tried to stay perfectly still and quiet. He could hear the men passing by. One walked right by. If that man was a half an inch over with his step, he would have been on Damien. He let out a sigh of relief when they passed by and out of sight.

Damien uncovered their bodies and carefully got up, cradling Esmeralda in his arms. She had been shot in the back and right through her heart. She was dead and as he sat there weeping for the loss of his beloved daughter, he had wished for the first time, for black magic. Maybe then he could have had a spell to bring her back. His weeps turned into sobs. His sunshine was gone. His faithful owl was perched once again on his shoulder letting out a squawk of sorrow.

Damien wiped his tear stained face. He knew he had to get out of there. Those men would be back. He turned to owl, "you must fly home. You must go. Katarina knows if you come home without us that there was trouble. She needs to know I won't be home for a while."

Owl let out a hoot and Damien watched as owl flew straight up and out of sight. He stood up, still cradling Esmeralda's lifeless body in his arms as he fought the woods once again. He had only gone a little way when something caught his eye. He laid Esmeralda against a tree and picked up the item. It must have dropped from one of the men. It was a pocket book of some kind. It had an animal hide cover and paper that only the rich could have. It was too dark to see anything in it so he stuck it in his pack and took a moment to listen. There were no sounds out of the ordinary just the sounds of the woods. He knew of another hide out just around the bend. He picked up Esmeralda and started walking hearing only the sounds of his heavy footsteps cracking the small twigs beneath the mossy ground cover.

It didn't take long before he found it. It was more hidden then the first. He carefully placed Esmeralda on the ground and made a fire. It was a smaller cave but it had to do. He untied the bear skin from the pack and carefully wrapped Esmeralda up in it and placed her against the back wall of the cave. He would give her the proper burial once he brought her home. Damien didn't look forward to that day. His beloved Katarina was going to take their daughters death very hard.

He knew he couldn't go back until he sought those out that killed her and as far as he was concerned that coven was also to blame. If they hadn't been running from those men, then they would have never crossed paths with them. They too will pay.

He pulled out the animal hide covered book and looked at it. It belonged to a man named Edward Guastella. *He shouldn't be too hard to find him. He had to have come from Messina,* he told himself as he started planning his revenge. Damien figured he knew where Edward would be so he focused on the witch coven that led the witch hunt into his path. He pulled out his book from the pack and page by page looked at every spell including the ones he shared with the others at the gathering. He didn't think any of the spells would be dark enough. He was always taught that his kind were only to do good, not harm.

He knew what he had to do. He had to find the witches of the black magic and he knew just where to look. He had to go north and it had to be at night. He went over to Esmeralda's body, uncovered her face and kissed her forehead.

"I'll be back. I promise," he said to her as he ran his hand along her face, "I will avenge your death, my daughter." He put the fire out and with great heaviness started out northbound.

Damien was able to cover ground very fast and even though it was early morning hours, it was still pitch black. He moved slower the closer to the north he got. He could sense the evil, and knew they weren't far. He had heard from the others at the gathering that these northern witches were so brutal that they could rip your heart out so fast that you could watch them eat it like an apple, watching them take the first bite before killing over dead. He found the storytelling both amusing and disheartening. His kind would never do such a foul thing but now hatred was consuming his thoughts and the once distinct line between good and evil was blurring.

It wasn't hard to find their camp. They didn't exactly hide. There were a number of make shift hut houses in a circle. He could also see what looked to be a cave and wondered if the head of the coven lived in there by how the huts surrounded it. It seemed eerily quiet. They must be out. He carefully maneuvered through the woods towards the cave. He inched along the side of the rock front with his back to the rocks and his eyes locked on the huts.

Something didn't seem right and he wished he had owl with him. He had hoped that they had called it a night but knew better then to let his guard down. He slid around the corner and into the cave, still keeping his back to the wall. He had all his senses on high alert. He was a bit surprised that they didn't have anything to alert them that a stranger was among them or maybe they already knew he was there. That thought didn't make him feel any better, sending chills down his back.

He inched further in and saw a flicking light at the end of the tunnel. Stopping abruptly, he tried to relax himself by shutting his eyes and concentrating on his surroundings. He was a little surprised that his power to project himself worked. He saw only one witch in the cave. As he got closer to the light he could hear her talking. At first it was a low mumble, but when he was right around the corner he could hear exactly what she was saying.

"I know your there. Show yourself," the woman's raspy voice beckoned.

Damien slowly came around the corner, looking around the room for any others he may have missed. She was the only one.

"You want revenge," she spoke again.

"Yes I do," Damien snarled angrily through clenched teeth.

"You came here to seek help with revenge, did you not?" She declared. She appeared very old, sitting in the corner wrapped in animal hide reading a book, possibly a spell book, never looking up.

"Yes," Damien answered. He didn't need to ask who she was, he knew. She was the eldest of the witches in this particular coven.

"Come, sit!" she demanded waving him over. He knew not to say no.

"What is it that you want exactly?" She voiced closing her book.

"I want to learn your ways. I want to find the witches that brought darkness upon my family. I want to be strong enough to take on anyone and never to be helpless again," he stated. He never wanted to be defenseless again.

"Are you not afraid to come here?" she inquired. She knew everything before he had even shown up. She saw it all unfold and also saw how the darkness changed him.

"No. I came with purpose. I just lost one of the most important persons in my life; I will make it my mission to seek out those that destroyed my world."

"Your heart does not pump red, but black instead."

"It does."

She slowly got up and walked behind him. He knew not to show fear. "Close your eyes," she instructed as she placed one hand on his back and the other on his chest. It didn't take long before he felt darkness wash over him. She took the love and pain from his heart and replaced it with hate and contempt. She whispered a spell into his ear and when she was done, he felt strong, invincible and nothingness.

"By the way, the ones that passed through and brought the hunters, they will be heading towards your home. They were told by a couple of my people that Udine was a safe haven," she baited.

He was forever in her debt for what she did, "what is it that you require in return?"

"Get rid of the Benandanti. You are now one of us. You are a Streghe now and forever," she boasted crassly.

"Understood," he bowed with gratitude.

"Molto bene," she accepted as she went over to a small table against the wall, opened a small wooden box and walked back to Damien. "Hold out your arms. Ora!"

He did as he was told. She put a leather band around one wrist and with the long sharp nail of her index finger she started cutting his arm. He gritted his teeth, trying not to yell out in pain while she chanted a spell in another language. Not Sicilian, not Italian, it was a language that he had never heard before. Her nail was like a hot iron rod that was just pulled from burning coals. His body tightened with the pain but he held himself strong.

"Impressive," she said when she finished. He looked down and saw a symbol that he only assumed to be that of the Streghe.

"With?" he asked as he watched her spit on her finger and rub it on the cut and then watched as the cut healed into a scar.

"No one before you has ever just sat there as you have without screaming in pain when I perform the initiation. You are the first. Una forte," she said with a sinister grin. "Now be on your way. Do not fail me, do not fail the Streghe."

"I won't," he assured and started to get up.

"I will call upon you from time to time and when I summons you, you will come or breathe no more."

"Understood," he said coldly as he left.

He made his way back to the cave in record time. He could feel strength he never had before. He laid down beside his daughter's body and wrapped his arms around her. He wanted so badly to see that warm glow, but knew anything warm was a thing of the past.

When he woke, he could see the daylight trying to invade the cave. It was time to start his new life. One of which he thought he would never live. He felt no hurt and when he looked at the bear rug that kept his daughter pure anger and rage boiled under his skin. He pulled out the animal hide book and looked through it. It had a list of all the people the villagers thought were witches and a list of the different places this Edward guy went. This should be easy. He dressed down to blend in with the villagers and left the cave.

It was much easier to maneuver through the woods with his strength and heightened senses. He would be a force to recon with. He knew that the villagers would know he wasn't from around the area but he had a plan.

He went to the area that he first sensed the witches in the woods and decided to leave the woods at that point. There were fields of vegetables and he could see the top of a white house. *Good place to start,* he thought. He walked through the corn field as to not be seen. He didn't hear any noise and figured no one was around. As he got closer to the other end of the row he was in, he could see an old small shack of a house and he suddenly got a vision of the tenants that were once there, the witches.

Damien looked around again and still no

one stirred about. He went over to the shack helping himself in. He saw their last days there and he saw that Edward lived in the white house. *Perfetto*, he breathed as he started to plot.

He made his way to the main house and saw three men on horses leaving. He helped himself inside there too. He closed his eyes and thought safe. In an instant he knew right where to go. The strong pull led him into the study and hiding behind the huge painting was the house safe. He helped himself to the contents and then sat down at the desk and drafted a letter, addressing it to Edward and stuck it into the safe. He walked through the rest of the house, going into each room. He found what appeared to be a nursery, and while in that room, it came to him, an evil plan to get even with the ones involved in the death of his amata figlia Esmeralda.

It was time for him to start his journey home. While packing up his belongings he realized he had to break the news of Esmeralda's death to his wife. He dreaded that more then anything. Esmeralda was Katarina's life.

The trip home was long and miserable and he had a long time to think and plot. As he neared Udine darkness washed over him. He felt hatred to his core and then he heard her, the old lady from the cave. Her voice was old and raspy, "remember what you need to do, they are there. Find them and bring me their hearts."

"I will," he thought back as the horse he was riding galloped down the long dirt road to his house.

Katarina took the news worse then

Damien thought. She fell into a deep depression and no matter what he tried, nothing worked. She tried to kill herself but with Damien by her side, it was unsuccessful. During the night on the third day home, Damien was woken by a voice he recently became acquainted with, and with more anger then he had ever felt, he spoke back, "Not now. I can not leave my wife. She needs me here."

The witch's old raspy voice showed no remorse. "Come or breathe no more," and suddenly the scar on his wrist began to burn as if he had just stuck his arm directly into a roaring fire. With harsh realization he kissed his wife as she slept, promising a quick return and begged she keep herself save until then.

He moved with quickness he thought was not possible, yet he knew the old witch had something to do with it. When he arrived, it looked exactly as it had the night his daughter perished. It was all too quiet and that was unsettling to him. He wondered where the coven had gone. He entered the cave cautiously only to find it empty. Suddenly a sound of hissing laughter filled his ears. He had a sinking feeling of despair. "You are truly one of us now," the wicked voice laughed, taunting him.

"Where are you? Why have you brought me here?" he yelled. The voice spoke no more.

It didn't make sense to Damien, the trip to Sicily, until he walked through the doors of his home to find his beloved wife's lifeless body hanging from a rafter beam in their bedroom. Whatever good may have been buried deep inside Damien died in that moment.

"They will all pay!" he scolded under his breath as he watched his loyal servant Salvator placed the last stone on her grave.

Chapter 2

USA- Present day

It was a bitterly cold, stormy day for the beginning of May in Salem Massachusetts, but Sarah didn't mind, not today. She looked around the bare shell of what had been her apartment for the past eight years. Most of her twenties consumed in the 650 square foot living area. Her lifestyle was outgrowing the small space and she was looking forward to the change she was embarking on. Owning her first home before the age of thirty was an accomplishment that was both fulfilling and bittersweet. Her parents weren't here to see her successes and that saddened her.

A torrential rain had passed over the area the night before soaking everything in its path. Sarah would have been stressed out had it not been for the help of her friend Jenny. They had packed up almost all of her belongings the night before and even parked the moving truck outside her new home, waiting to be unpacked. Sarah was waiting anxiously for a phone call from the realtor. She walked over to the last box in the apartment, taped it up and took it out to her car. It took a few hard pushes to get the trunk closed. Sarah was determined to make it fit. She took one last look around the quiet neighborhood. The streets were still wet with pockets of puddles strewn about. It had been a very peculiar night weather wise. She could hear her cell phone ringing from inside the apartment and quickly ran to answer it.

"Hello?"

"Sarah, this is Mrs. Santes. I should be at the house in about 30 minutes. Will that work for you?" the realtor asked.

"Yes. I'll see you there," Sarah said smiling. She was so excited. No more apartment living for her. After they hung up, Sarah glanced around the empty apartment as she shut the door. She couldn't get out of there fast enough.

She had been in love with her new house since the first time seeing it three months ago and often found herself driving by it, hoping to one day own it. Today was that day. It all seemed so surreal to her. She didn't get very far before hitting gridlock due to an accident, but she was determined not to let it bother her. She refused to be in a bad mood today. Sarah turned the radio on; hoping to find upbeat music but a song that reminded her of her parents came on. Her eyes filled with tears. She fell into deep thoughts of the last few years her parents were alive.

She remembered being seven and her parents fought all the time. On weekends she would stay at her best friend Jenny's house. She loved it there. Jenny's parents treated her like one of their own children and there were many nights Sarah wished she had been. She hated her parents fighting. She would go to sleep many nights crying thinking it was her fault that they fought so much.

It had gotten so bad that most of the week was spent at her uncle's house. She hated it there. He made a point to make her aware that she was a hassle to have there. All he did was drink, snort lines of white powder and yell at her. When she tried to tell her parents, they wouldn't listen. They were too busy fighting. One night, while at her uncle's house, he was throwing a party. He and his friends were very drunk. She was in a back bedroom sleeping when one of the friends came in stumbling. He proceeded to touch her. She was terrified and cried all night. She only told one person, her friend Jenny.

It was years later when more bad things had happened. Sarah's parents had tried to work things out many times but their marriage was on the brink of divorce. On a last ditch effort, they decided to go away together to try one last time to work it out. Sarah wanted to stay the week at Jenny's house but her parents refused and made her stay with her aunt. Her aunt was a far better choice then her uncle. She let her talk to Jenny on the phone whenever she wanted. Then tragedy struck. She would never forget the day. It was a Sunday afternoon and she had been watching the clock, knowing her parents were due back and eager to see if they had worked everything out, besides she wanted to go home to her own room. Her parents told her they would be back no later then five o'clock. That time came and went. It was around ten at night when there was a knock on her aunt's door. She sat quietly at the top of the staircase waiting to see who it was but given the time she knew it couldn't have been good. She wondered who she would be living with.

"Oh God, no!" her aunt cried as she started to collapse but someone reached out and caught her. Sarah couldn't see who it was but saw the shirt. It was a police officer. *What is going on*, she panicked as she felt herself running down the stairs.

"Auntie Serena what's the matter?" Sarah's heart was racing.

"Oh Sarah," She sobbed grabbing a hold of Sarah squeezing her tight.

What she was about to be told would shatter her world. The police left Serena's house and she led Sarah into the living room and sat her down. She didn't know quite how to tell Sarah so she just told her point blank. Sarah was devastated. The next few weeks were a blur to her. She remembered sitting in the cold watching her parents caskets being lowered into the ground, watching as people came up to comfort her days after, packing her things and lasting only another couple of weeks with her aunt before her aunt had asked Jenny's parents to take her in. Serena didn't want a constant reminder of her sister around. Sarah felt like trash that kept getting put out. Jenny's parents felt so bad for the little girl they decided to take her in as their own. Jenny loved the idea of Sarah being like a sister.

The sound of a few car horns brought her out of the trance she was in. She realized that the cars in front of her had moved and she had failed to follow suit. She waved her hand in her review mirror at the honking car behind her and quickly caught up to the other cars and back to a stand still.

"OH COME ON! DAMN!" Sarah yelled at the cars in front of her. "What is the hold up?" she huffed as she looked in her rear view mirror, catching the driver behind her hitting his steering wheel. It made her laugh. She looked at the time, *better call the realtor.*

"Hello?" Mrs. Santes asked.

"Hi, it's Sarah."

"Oh I'm glad you called. I am tied up in bad traffic and I'm running a little late."

"Yah, me too. That's why I was calling." Sarah said chuckling at the coincidence.

"Ok, well I guess we will see each other at the house when we get there," Mrs. Santes stated.

"Sounds good," Sarah said as they hung up. She picked up her thoughts where she had left off. Sarah fell into a dark place after the death of her parents. The popular kids at school put her in the "Goth" category but Jenny wouldn't allow any of them to pick on her like they did with others. Jenny was a cheerleader and one of the most popular kids on campus but even still, Jenny never treated Sarah any different. 'Tight friends until the end' she always told Sarah.

Other then Jenny, Sarah became friends with what the teachers deemed the "bad kids":

the loners, the misfits, the stoners, the ones from broken homes and the rockers, and although she didn't really fit in with them, they were more excepting then the jocks and cheerleader types. One time Sarah was pulled out of class and sent to the school counselor's office just to be told by him, that given her up bringing, the chances of her succeeding in life was less then 5%. She couldn't believe what she was hearing and responded with a 'gee thanks' and went back to class.

Sarah only had a handful of friends in high school and she did only what she had too to get through those years. It wasn't easy for her by any means, she had the pressures of grades, fitting in, being teased, getting cruel jokes played on her, getting stood up at all the high school dances including prom all the while dealing with nightmares of her dead parents and of the dark shadow that taunts her at the foot of her bed during the night.

Jenny's parents even had her see a counselor that was recommended by their family doctor. Not because he thought something was wrong with her, but to help her with her nightmares and the things that have happened to her.

In the end, Sarah graduated and went on to an Ivy League college. She received her Bachelors in Business Management and as one of her electives, she chose a history class. It was during that class she got started in doing a family tree in hopes she could stretch back a hundred years or so. It was also then that she became fascinated in research, of any kind. She knew it would be hard to go back a hundred years but after doing a research paper on Italy, she grew obsessed at the idea that her ancestors could have had a part in Italy's history. Sarah stayed focused on her studies and if she had any free time, which wasn't often, she worked on a very long process of piecing together the history of her family's name.

After she graduated with honors, she took a much needed vacation to Italy. She didn't make it to Sicily, but vowed she would in the next few years. She had fallen in love with Tuscany and the country side, staying at B&B's rather then hotels. It felt more inviting at a B&B, more of a personal touch plus she learned more about the area at the morning breakfasts from the others there. The five day trip went by way too fast and she felt a little cheated. *Next time, ten days at least*, she thought. She couldn't wait to come back, she felt very at ease and she hadn't had one nightmare.

Sarah was going to talk Jenny in coming back with her, if she could but Jenny was busy being courted by a guy that had been waiting to date her for quite some time. Jenny had finally given in.

After coming back from Italy, Sarah decided to get into the dating scene thanks to a push from her friends, who have managed to settle down over the course of her college days. Relationships didn't come easy for her, sometimes struggling to put more effort into them then she should have or maybe it was because of her childhood that she felt disconnected from the intimacy that a relationship should have. Sarah had just accepted the fact that she is damaged goods, but she went on dates, her friends set up for her, to please them. But to be perfectly honest, she was growing tired of it.

She had an entry level position in what Forbes considered an up and coming business. The company took care of their employees. The company was called Global Research Inc. It claimed to be the biggest research company on the market and could do the job better and faster then any other research company. The company was only five years old when Sarah joined them, it was her dream job.

She would work on her family name when she had time to but didn't do too much in fear of getting in trouble. It was said that the company monitored the computers and the sites workers used. Yes, the company took care of their employees, but it came at a price of working long hours. Sarah didn't mind though, it kept her busy. Her hard work did pay off, although at the expense of losing some friends along the way, never having the time for them but again she didn't mind. The older she was getting the more recluse, the more "in my own little world" she became. Jenny's mom's voice played in her head, telling her, "it's not normal or healthy to live that way!" She loved that Jenny's parents considered her as a daughter and Jenny always introduced her as her sister. It made her feel loved.

Sarah broke from her reminiscing to look at the time, *ugghhh;* she just wanted to get to her new house. The ride across town seemed never ending with the horrible traffic, possibly the worse she had ever seen it. She was about half way there. *Wonder if Mrs. Mantes has made it there yet,* Sarah decided to send her a text letting her know she was almost there. Mrs. Mantes sent her one back saying she had just gotten there and not to worry and to be safe.

A song came on the radio that reminded Sarah of a particular day at work. The boss above Sarah's boss, Mr. Davis, called her into his office. She didn't know what was going on. She hadn't seen her boss, Mr. Adams, all morning and it was now after lunch. She was hoping she wasn't going to get in trouble for working on her own research. She had always gotten her work done ahead of schedule.

"Sir, you wanted to see me?" She stood nervously at Mr. Davis's door.

"Yes, come in, shut the door behind you and have a seat." He instructed. He was a very distinguished man, always dressed like he just stepped out of the G.Q. magazine. He continued, "I wanted to personally tell you before I sent out a memo that Mr. Adams is no longer employed with us. And with that said, I wanted to give you first choice to step into his place."

The look on her face must have been some sight, and with a slight grin, he went on. "Yes, that means a promotion and a raise. You will also have his old office and the same expense account plus you will be traveling for hands on, in person kind of research. What do you think about that?"

She didn't have to think about it, she already loved what she did, so the offer was icing on the cake. Without hesitation, Sarah said yes. Mr. Davis gave her the rest of the day off to clean out her desk and move her stuff into her new office, and to get an early start on the weekend.

She had met a few friends to celebrate that Friday night and decided then that she would drag herself out every Friday night just so she could tell Jenny's mom, as a rebuttal, that she was social.

A year later, here she was, almost to the house she was about to call her very own. She felt accomplished. At that moment, she thought about that school counselor who said she wouldn't amount to much...*what did he know*.

She pulled into the driveway behind Mrs. Mantes's car. She got out and stopped halfway up the walkway, stood there a moment staring at her new house. It was surreal moment. A rush of pride washed over her. She took a quick look around. The entire house looked perfect, except the one next to hers. It gave her the creeps, but shrugged it off, *no one lived there so of course it would look like it did*, she thought. She walked into the house to find Mrs. Mantes waiting in the kitchen.

"Sorry it took so long. I don't think I have ever seen it so bad out there," Sarah stated apologetically.

"I understand. So here it is. You sign on the dotted line of this final paper and this beautiful house is all yours," Mrs. Mantes said with a big smile. Sarah with a bigger smile snagged the pen off the counter and signed her name as fast as she could.

"Congratulations Sarah Guastella! You now own this home!" Mrs. Mantes shouted like a game show host while shaking Sarah's hand. Sarah couldn't help but laugh. After the realtor left, Sarah unpacked her car, going slowly through each room of her new home. Her smile got bigger with each one. She called Jenny.

"Hello chicka" Jenny said when she answered.

"IM A HOMEOWNER!!!" Sarah excitedly shouted. She could hear Jenny laugh.

"Good I'll be right over. We have to celebrate!" Jenny said.

"Is Robert out of town?" Sarah questioned.

"Yep!" Jenny answered laughing.

"Ok then why aren't you here yet?" Sarah joked sarcastically.

"I'm on my way!" Jenny laughed as she hung up.

Twenty minutes later Jenny was bouncing through the door holding two bottles of wine which they drank as they christened each room with a toast. Jenny took pictures of Sarah in every room and a few outside as well to mark such a big moment, a good moment in what had been a rough life.

It didn't take Sarah long to settle in and get down a routine. It was pretty basic, work, gym, sometimes the store then home. She spent a lot of time on the computer doing research for work or on her family name. She found a self-proclaimed, best-in-the-business genealogist and turned over all the information she had thus far to him. She had hit a dead end.

Her life was so basic that some would say it was lifeless for how young she was but it suited her just fine; except for the nightmares. Back when Sarah was younger and Jenny's parents made her see a psychiatrist, her nightmares always seemed to become the topic of conversation. The psychiatrist said it would help to write the nightmares down; that it could be the key in stopping them, *boy was she wrong*, Sarah thought. She overheard the psychiatrist say that she thought Sarah conjured up the "nightmares" due to her parents death coupled with the trauma she suffered as a child. Sarah was very happy when those sessions ended.

Chapter 3

Sarah eyes popped open, it was dark and quiet, and in the middle of the night. She knew it was due to another nightmare but she couldn't remember a thing. Panic swept over her when she realized she couldn't move. Her head could move but from neck down her body felt like cement. She tried to yell but nothing came out, her mouth didn't move. *What is going on? What's wrong with me?* Panic and fear set in.

She hears something at the foot of her bed and quickly scanned the room seeing that something even darker then the darkness of the room was moving towards the side of her bed. *What the hell is that!!?* She tried yelling but again nothing, just the voice in her head. The dark thing was moving so slow up the side of the bed towards her. Closer and closer it came but she couldn't make out what it was. Everything was in slow motion except the feeling of sheer terror inside of her. Her heart was pounding so hard it was all she could hear. She could feel her eyes widen as she realized that it was right beside her. With her heart pounding so hard she was having a hard time catching her breath. She started to feel tears running down the sides of her face. The voice in her head was screaming, but for no one to hear. *What do you want? What are you?* Her mouth won't open and nothing was working. In a split second, the thing grabbed her hand and in the darkness all she can see are blinding white, sharp teeth and as they sink into her fingers, she lets out a blood shrieking scream.

With a big gasp of breath, as if her head had been submerged in water and let out just as she was drawing her last breath, her eyes opened as wide as they could, heart still pounding as she tried to catch her breath. She can still feel the tears running down her face, afraid to move, she just laid in her bed, staring at the ceiling. Slowly her breathing returns to a normal pace, although her heart was still racing but the pounding was not as hard as it had been.

She could feel excruciating pain on her right hand but she was too afraid to look. *"Look at your hand,"* her mind commanded, *"get up and deal with it!"*

She pulled herself and her thoughts together just enough to slowly raise her hand, horrified to see why it's hurting so bad. There's nothing. *Nothing, what the hell?* She studied every inch of her hand, but nothing. She made a fist, and then opened it. Nothing was wrong. "Am I going crazy?" She asked herself.

Slowly, she sat up and looked around the room. Nothing was out of place. Her breathing and heart rate were almost back to normal. She let out a big sigh and figured she better get on with her day. She has had this nightmare many times before but this was by far the worst. *Why did that nightmare get so bad?* She pondered. Periodically, she would look over her hand half expecting to see bite marks, but nothing. Still, it sent chills down her back.

The day went off without a hitch. After work she did her usual routine, worked out at the gym, a quick stop at the grocery store and then spent the evening vegging out in front of the TV. She dreaded going to bed in fear of a repeat from the night before. But eventually she had too; she couldn't keep her eyes open any longer. It wouldn't last.

Her eyes popped open and instantly horror, fear and panic washed over her, and again she couldn't move and again tears were running down the sides of her face. The voice inside her head was screaming at the dark shadowy thing but only she could hear it. She tried real hard to focus on it trying to make out what it was other then a shade of dark, darker then the night. This time it stayed at the foot of the bed taunting her, moving back and fourth, gliding as if on air.

"What do u want?" her inner voice yelling out, tears streaming down her face, partly from frustration but mostly from the fear of the not knowing who, what or why this was happening. Again, she wakes in the same way as the night before, sweating, heart pounding, rapid breathing, and slight confusion. This experience continues for days that turned into weeks. The only difference from the first night to the nights following is that the dark thing continues to only taunt her. She settled into and accepted what had become a routine. She dreaded going to sleep every night knowing it would be the same as the last. She fought it as long as she could but always succumbed to the heaviness that took a hold of her eyes.

It was a month later and again Sarah struggled with going to sleep. The bags under her eyes had formed bags. This night would be different. Had she known how different, she wouldn't have fought so hard to stay awake. She woke again in a panic, not at the hands of the dark thing lurking about her room but because the alarm clock had gone off. It was light out. She had slept through the night without a visit from the dark thing. *What a relief*, she thought. To her surprise, she was a little disturbed by it. Just when she started thinking it was a nightly occurrence, it changed. She started her day hopeful that at nights end to have a repeat of the night before. She would be wrong.

She made plans that evening to meet up with her friends for dinner and cocktails. It was nice. For the first time in weeks she was able to keep her mind off the nightmare. They talked and laughed late into the night. It was around 1 a.m. and they knew the lounge would be closing and they wanted to leave before the lounge started pushing the rest of the party goers out. They were saying their goodbyes and settling the tab when a rush of fear came over her. The same fear she had grown accustomed too.

"But I'm not asleep," She heard herself say out loud.

"What was that Sarah?" asked Jenny. Jenny was now married and to one of the wealthiest business men in the city, but thankfully that didn't change who Jenny was, a free spirit, give u the shirt off her back kind of person. Sarah admired her for that.

Sarah shook her head as she answered, "Nothing, just thinking out loud," giving a half hearted smile as she glanced around. Nothing out of the ordinary, just the typical before closing bar scene, people hurrying to close out their tabs, half drunk people bumping into others as they try to get their coats on and men trying a last ditch effort in picking up women for a quick early a.m. romp. Her eyes had almost made it completely around the lounge until she caught something in her peripheral vision that didn't fit the scene, something dark and moving. But when Sarah looked in that direction, there was nothing. Still a little shaken from earlier, she agreed to walk out with the remaining friend hoping the panic in her voice wasn't noticed.

Once into her car, Sarah took in a few deep breathes to calm herself, a technique she learned in a yoga class that she attempted to take years ago. It worked, she felt much calmer. *What do u know? Useful*, she smiled at the thought of herself in some of the yoga posses she attempted. It made her chuckle. Home she went.

As she pulled into her driveway she couldn't help but notice a big yellow moving truck outside the vacant house next to hers. She didn't remember seeing the truck there earlier, but she had stopped paying attention to the dark and gloomy house some time ago, except to curse at the un-manicured lawn every time she had mowed her own. That house had sat vacant for so long it didn't look as alive and inviting as the rest of the houses on the street. She had hoped the new owners would change that. Sarah hadn't realized that she had stopped half way up the walkway to her porch and had been starring at the dark house in some bizarre trance.

Something by the moving truck caught her eye. She turned her head quickly to see what it was, and there he stood. It was dark and she couldn't make out any more then to see he was tall with dark hair. He was dressed in dark clothing with his arms down at his side, starring back at her, still as could be. She heard a noise from behind her and it made her jump, spinning around quickly to see what it was. A cat came from around the other side of her car. *"Stupid cat"* she huffed, her heart racing, then looked back in the direction of who she could only assume to be her new neighbor, but he was gone. She thought how odd it was that she hadn't heard him walk away, didn't hear the sound of any doors shutting. Sarah looked at the dark house and thought again how weird it was that no lights were on. She let out a little sigh as she made her way to her house and went in. She was tired, it was a long day and she just wanted to go to bed. She didn't think about the nightmare, she didn't care, either because of how tired she was or because she had a good buzz going thanks to the alcohol. The only thing she was thinking about was that she shouldn't have driven home in her current condition.

She changed into her pajamas and as she turned off the light in her bedroom a loud noise came from outside, startling her. She went over to the window and peaked out of the little crack between the curtains. Her neighbor was closing up the back of the moving truck. All of a sudden, with eerie quickness he turned his head and looked straight up at her. She let out a gasp and jumped back.

"Crazy, he couldn't have seen me," the words escaped her mouth in disbelief. She wanted so badly to believe that he didn't see her, as if she was a peeping Tom. Something about the way he looked at her sent chills down her back and fear through her body. With more caution, she took a step forward and peaked through the curtain again. She could feel her heart starting to beat a little harder. He was gone.

With a deep sigh of relief she stepped back, got into bed and pulled the blankets up to her neck, holding on to them tightly. Little did she know, he was right across from her window, looking back at her through his window, and little did she know that as soon as she fell asleep, the dark thing would be back. She relaxed into her bed, more at ease, more hopeful that she would have yet another good night's sleep following such a great day. Sleep was more inviting to her and before she knew it her eyes closed.

"*Oh God! Not again,*" the voice in her head cried as she stared wide eyed at the ceiling. It's still dark and she couldn't move. She moved her eyes to focus on the foot of her bed. The usual darkness, and then, there it was. The dark shadow moved back and fourth taunting her. The voice in her head began yelling in horror.

"What do you want from me? Leave me alone!" It was then that she realized she was actually yelling it. Her lips were moving, hearing her own voice squeaking even though it sounded faint next to the pounding in her chest. It stopped, looked her way, turned and slowly started making its way up the side of her bed.

"What do you want!" she demanded to know.

"Who are you? What are you?" It seemingly ignored her demands.

"What the hell do you want?" She heard herself scream again.

It stopped next to her and slowly turned to face her. Even in the darkness, she saw something that washed horror throughout her entire body; it smiled revealing a bright white smile, exposing sharp teeth she had seen before. She started sobbing hard, her body frozen, heavy like cement. Through her tears she asked one more time. "What do you want?"

It leaned down by the side of her head and in almost a whisper said in a low deep voice, "YOU!" Panic, fear, and horror consumed her entire body.

Beep, beep, beep, beep, the sound of her alarm clock woke her up. She laid in her bed sobbing, her heart racing, *why?* She wondered. *What did it mean?* She could feel the tears running down the sides of her cheeks toward her ears but she didn't care, she didn't move, until she felt pain. *Ouch! What the hell!* The salty tears hit her right ear, stinging it. When she wiped her ear with her hand, she felt more pain. Something wasn't right. She looked at her hand, finding blood on it; she darted out of her bed to her desk and looked in the mirror. *Oh my God*! There was a hole in her ear lobe, bigger than the average earring hole. Panic came over her again. *It bit me! No way.* She reached for the phone and started dialing then stopped. *Who am I going to call? Who would listen to me and not think I have lost my mind? If anyone asks I'll just tell them an earring must have ripped out during the night,* convincing herself a more logical reason.

She stood in front of her desk looking in the mirror. *What is going on?* She started to tear up again and looked down shaking her head. *No, no, I can't think of this right now.* Sitting on her desk, under her hand, was a folder with the start of her research into her families past. It had sat untouched for the past few months. She went into the bathroom, bandaged up her ear and went back to the desk. She opened up the folder to get her mind on something different. She had hit a dead end not long after starting the search and at one point she had turned it over to a genealogist but after a few weeks of no return calls, she went to his office to find that he had passed away of unknown causes a few days after meeting with her.

Sarah took the folder with her to work in hopes of finding a new genealogist to help her. *A good distraction*, she thought. She had already put way too much time and energy into this project to give up now. She managed to trace her family's ancestors back to a small town in Sicily. Her aunt had warned her to be careful, when she first learned Sarah was looking into the family line, but when Sarah questioned her aunt about that, her aunt only played it off as a joke because of them being Sicilian. *"Mobs and all, you know!"* Sarah didn't buy it. She felt her aunt was hiding something more.

She had hit a wall and with the nightmares coming on a regular basis, she didn't have the mindset to concentrate on research that she wasn't getting paid for.

After work she got in touch with a new genealogist a co-worker told her about. He said to stop by one day in the next week and he would be happy to start on it. She had called him from the road and was a little disappointed that he wouldn't see her now. She didn't really want to go home, not because she didn't like her house but because she wasn't sure what was going on there. *This is crazy,* she thought. She wasn't going to let this dark thing scare her into not enjoying a house she worked so hard to get. As she pulled into the driveway she looked over at the dark house. "*Maybe I should go over and introduce myself...*" she thought as she noticed again that there were no signs of life. "*Maybe not,*" as usual it was dark. She let out a sigh and decided for now to go inside and make dinner. It was Friday afternoon. *What am I going to do for the next two days? No work, No family history to work on, and all my friends are busy with their families,* she huffed suddenly feeling lonely.

She made dinner and took it into the living room where she had a movie playing. She had all the lights off except the porch and hall lights and before long it was dark outside. She became bored and restless and found herself standing in her dark kitchen looking around. *Aahhh a bottle of wine, perfect.* She grabbed the bottle from the wine rack on the counter and turned to go towards the glass cupboard and froze. Chills went down her back. It was her neighbor standing outside her kitchen window starring at her. She jumped back as fear took over, and flipped on the light. He was gone. Her inner voice couldn't stay quiet. *Was that really him or my mind playing tricks on me?*

"Stop it stupid, it was only your mind," she said disgusted at herself. She grabbed a glass and the bottle and headed back into the living room; flipping the light off as she went out. What she failed to see was that as soon as she had turned the light off, he was there, watching her through the window, watching her every move.

As the movie was ending she reached for the bottle of wine. *"Damn, empty. That went down way to easy."* She gave in and decided to head upstairs and as she entered her room her eyes looked across the room to the window. Curiosity got the better of her and she left the light off and walked over to the window and peaked out again towards the dark house. She looked at the window straight across from hers, nothing but darkness. She could see a faint light coming from the back side of the house. *It figured that the only person to buy such a dark house would be dark himself,* voicing her displeasure. Just as she was about to step away from the window a light from the room directly across from her came on. She couldn't see anything more then what was seen in the crack of the curtains. She didn't want to get caught by moving the curtains and even then still found herself standing off to one side and peeking through.

She could see shadows of someone moving about the room. At that moment she told herself that she was going to introduce herself one day to the mysterious man that lived next door. Just as she was about to move away from the window, he came into sight. It was a profile shot of him. He looked perfect. She again found herself in a trance but knew to move away, she was so afraid of getting caught. She decided to go back to watching television. He on the other hand was watching her from his window and as he turned away to leave his room a slight smirk come across his face.

Chapter 4

She doesn't know that he has come for her, that he is the one who haunts her at night. He watches her through her windows and has been caught a couple of times but in ways that would make her think it's only her mind playing tricks on her. This amuses him in a dark twisted way, the cat and mouse game he is playing with her, a game she doesn't know she is playing.

If she only knew the danger she was facing, the danger she put herself in by looking into her family's past, he knew, he was there because of it. He had to settle a score. He didn't know her and it didn't matter. He hated everything about her, hated what her family stood for, she will pay. He will settle the score for his family, he will end this horrible curse, he didn't like being this way, and he didn't like what he had become because of her family. He had waited for so long to end this bloody curse, so long for someone to show up. He wasn't going to let this opportunity get away from him. He didn't want to be a freak, it wasn't something he chose to be, it was her ancestors that did this but it will end with her. He thinks to himself as he watches her from behind the sheer black curtains in his living room, she almost backs into her own garbage can, "Stupid woman," he thought and the sound of the phone ringing breaks his trance on her.

"Soon!" he spoke in a low irritated voice, "I will fix this, promise," hanging up abruptly. He swiped his keys off the counter and off he went. Good thing he knew her schedule, made it easier to keep tabs on her. *She really needs to change her schedule up,* he thought, *"dumb woman."* As usual he found her car parked in roughly the same spot as the day before outside her work. Predictable. He knew she would be there for at least the next 7 hours. He had time. He went back to his house, parked the car back in the garage, went to the hall closet, grabbed a little black bag and went out the back door. He glanced around to make sure no one saw him and quickly went to the back door of her house. With the help of the little black bag the lock was very easy. He shut the door behind him making sure to leave no prints. She keeps a very clean and tidy house and the décor was very nice. *"What a waste"* he spoke.

He started looking in the drawers of the kitchen. Nothing. He opened the refrigerator, *"Hhmm.* Wow, should have known," he spoke in a snarky tone. Everything in it was evenly spaced, nice and tidy. He took a bottle of water and shut the door. This amused him. He made his way to the living room, studying the room. He never really paid much attention to this room before. He was a little surprised; the inside wasn't as bright and cheery as the outside of her house. Darker colors. If it wasn't for the fact that he was there to end the curse and the fact that he was suppose to hate her, he would almost be compelled to take her out. He made his way upstairs. He knew the layout well. He frequents this house often at night.

He went to the desk in her room, *there has to be something in here,* he thought as he riffled through the papers, pens, and paper clips. *Nothing of use.* He made his way over to the nightstand, being careful to leave everything as he finds it. He started with the nightstand on the opposite side from where she sleeps. Books about vampires. *"How original"* shaking his head in disgust, he snarled. The other nightstand proved more interesting. A journal... *hmmm....* He glanced at the clock seeing he had time and decided to lay down where he had watched her lay while taunting her. He opened up the journal and started reading. The first page was dated almost a year ago. He flipped forward and looked at the last entry- last night- the journal almost full. He flipped back to page 1 and began to read it...

It's about 3 am and again I have woken up due to a nightmare. I can't remember it, just that I woke up with my heart racing...stupid therapist anyway. Keep a journal, she said, it will keep the nightmares away, she said... what crap! It's been about 15 years of writing in a journal and it hasn't worked. So frustrated with it all. Why am I having these scary nightmares.. What is the meaning behind it? What is this dark thing haunting me?

"Haunting her?" he breathed. "I've only just started to mess with her." He skipped ahead a few pages and continued reading...

"Wonder if I'll ever find someone... All my friends have settled down, some even have children. What is wrong with me? I live a very routine life, work, and home and occasionally go out with my

friends, no spark, no excitement.... Every night ending the same way; Alone. Only my thoughts to keep me company. Maybe I should get a dog. No. No. Bad idea, can't keep a plant alive. It's not like I don't go out on dates, there's nothing wrong with the men, there's just nothing on my part and I'm not willing to settle......"

He flipped forward to the last entry dated the day before. *Hmm, should be good*, he hoped.

"I woke last night again to find that thing taunting me at the end of my bed. Really wish it would stop. I wonder what it meant by wanting me. I feel as though there has been this cloud of darkness looming over me. Wish I knew why. Well hopefully that new genealogist can make head way in my ancestors; at least it could possibly give me something to fill the nights and weekends up with.

There's a new neighbor next to me, he is very mysterious, there's a sense of darkness and fear seems to creep through me but I find myself intrigued by him. I find myself peaking though my curtains in his direction in hopes to get a glimpse of him. Don't know what it is that I'm drawn too. Even thought I saw him once outside my kitchen window but it was my mind playing tricks on me. I never see him come or go. No lights on at night accept a couple of times. I swear he has caught me looking, but there's no way he could have seen me- at least I hope not. I hope I don't have another nightmare tonight, OK well bored with this, will write in you tomorrow."

He shut the book, *interesting; she is drawn to me even though she senses fear. This may be easier then I thought.* He sat up and swung his legs over the side of the bed. He looked to see what else was in the nightstand; nothing. He went through her closets and the dresser drawers, nothing. He went into the master bathroom. There was a picture hanging on the wall that caught his attention. It was old. The picture itself was something he had seen many times before. He swept his hand over it. It was of Sicily. He missed being home, minus the nagging family. He looked through the rest of her bathroom; noting how spotless it was and finding himself approving this quality about her. He saw a night shirt hanging on the back of the door. He grabbed it and held it up to his face, it had her scent on it and to his surprised he liked it. That made him mad. He had to stay focused on how he was going to get revenge and break the curse for his family. He left her bedroom, making his way back to the back door, still holding her shirt and making sure that everything was exactly how he found it. He had lost track of time and spent way more time then he wanted in her house. Just as he shut the door, she was opening the front door.

That was too close; he won't make that mistake again. He quickly went back to his house without anyone seeing him. Still holding her night shirt, he put away the little black bag, and headed upstairs.

He laid her shirt down on his bed and pulled an old chest out of the bottom of the closet. He opened it up and moved some things around, folded up the shirt, put it in and closed it back up. He looked at the time, *shoot*. He had to get ready. She would be leaving soon, although he did know where she was going, it was Friday after all. He decided to take his time. He didn't want to leave before she did. He started backing out of his driveway when he noticed her car was still parked in her driveway. *Hmmm, she is normally gone by now.*

"Great, that changes things," he said out loud as he drove back into the garage. Hopefully no one saw him do that. He looked around before shutting the door, didn't seem so. Irritated, he wondered why she hadn't left. He pulled a small notebook out of a drawer in the kitchen and wrote down her change. He had been documenting her every move and this was out of character. He was planning a visit tonight, but with her not going out, that may change. He was drawn to her, but he thought it was out of hatred and he was hell bent on breaking the curse.

He went upstairs and pulled out the chest from the closet and opened it. He grabbed the old leather bound journal and started thumbing through it, stopping to read a page here and there. The expression on his face changed from emptiness and anger to sadness. The journal had been passed down through the generations and if he can not succeed in breaking the curse it will get passed on to the next male in the family line. It was his understanding from the journal that only a male in the family with direct linage could break the curse, and obviously the ones before him had failed. The curse doesn't hit every male; it has skipped generations, although from the looks of the journal entries, not many.

He hated what her ancestors did to his and wondered how different it would have been had the curse not happened. The only positive thing from it was that he was very wealthy, thanks to his abilities. He was thankful that his family was still back in Italy. He loves them dearly but grew tired of the constant nagging about the curse. He finds himself avoiding the calls from home. He closed the book and put it back in the chest. He picked up an old animal hide pouch and emptied the contents into his hand. There was an old heavy silver medallion with the symbol of what he thought had to do with his ancestors, just didn't know if it was before or after the curse so he didn't wear it and the symbol didn't match the symbol on the ring he wore, which was post curse.

He never really read the journal other then to skim through it and the parts he had read said nothing about the medallion. He never really cared about the items in the chest before but over the last few years he has felt more compelled to. He looked down and her night shirt caught his eyes, and in an instant rage came over him. He threw the animal hide pouch back into the chest and slammed the lid down shoving the chest back into the closet.

He wondered what she was up to. He went out the back door to his house and crossed over into hers. He could see lights on in her bedroom and living room. He peaked into her kitchen window. *Damn her*, she had put a curtain up in the window. *She must have done that after she got spooked.* He let out a whisper of a chuckle. *Good.* He went around to the side of her house and again curtains drawn in all the windows. Just then the lights went out in her house. He heard the garage door open. *She's leaving?* He ran back into his house, swiped his keys and notebook and headed out, irritated once again by the change.

Even though she was already out of sight by the time he was on the road, he knew where to find her. He was right. He backed into the space opened next to the driver's side of her car. He knew that the bold move was pushing it but she didn't know what he drove and he didn't care. She was at the usual Friday night hangout. The dinner portion of the evening must have been cancelled. This is where her and her friends come for cocktails.

He was able to get into her car without a problem, of course. The car still had her scent lingering in the air. He went through the glove box and center consol but there was nothing, the car, like her house, was squeaky clean. Just as he was getting out of her car he noticed a business card for a genealogist. *Hmm*. He took down the information and put the card back.

She was sitting at a table with four other women. They were all laughing and seemingly having a good time. He found an empty bar stool on the other side of the bar, next to the wall, the lighting was dimmer there, *perfect, wont be seen there*. After watching her for a short time she got up and headed towards the bathroom. As soon as she left the table and had her back to her friends, she stopped smiling. She looked like she didn't want to be there but going through the motions anyway.

He knew what that felt like, he had to do that back home in Italy and that made him angry. He followed her but stayed back enough not to be seen. He pushed open the women's restroom door just a crack. It sounded like only one person was in there, her. *Good start the night early*, he thought with a sinister grin.

As she sat in the stall she heard the other stall doors being slammed open. It made her jump, fear set in and her heart began to race.

Without thinking, and out of reaction, she put her feet up in the air and froze, trying not to breathe. She heard the one on her left open, hers was next. She closed her eyes and held her breath. Nothing. The one on her right slammed opened instead and continued all the way down to the last one. *Why was mine skipped?* She looked up, nothing. She looked through the cracks of the door, couldn't see anything. Not even a shadow of a person moving around. She was afraid to leave and waited for someone to come in before she left the stall. It seemed to take forever. A couple of women came in together, they obviously were having a good night, maybe even had a few too many cocktails and she envied that. She got herself composed enough to leave the stall. She went to the counter and gave herself a once over in the mirror. The women took the last two stalls of the restroom, talking and laughing together, which made her relax. She ran her hands under the water in the sink and looked down at them. *Shaking was almost gone.* She looked back up at the mirror and saw a dark figure standing in the opened stall directly behind her. She jumped and whipped around but nothing was there. She must have yelled because the two women came rushing out of their stalls.

"Are you ok?" one asked

"Yeess, yes I am. I'm fine. I thought I saw something behind me when I looked in the mirror but it was just the way the stall door was open. Sorry I didn't realize I was that loud." She could feel her cheeks getting red with embarrassment.

"No problem," as they giggled back. Feeling completely stupid she left the restroom and headed back to her friends. As she walked towards the table she saw the women who were just in the restroom laughing with their friends and pointing in her direction. *Great*, she huffed. She made it back to her table and took a seat. Jenny being observant noticed Sarah's behavior.

"Your face is red, are you ok?" Jenny asked.

"Yes, just a little warm." she didn't want them to think she was losing her mind and knew they would if she told them what has been happening to her.

He was back on the bar stool watching her reaction to what just happened. It pleased him immensely to see her coming apart but trying so hard to keep it together. *Just wait until tonight.*

Chapter 5

Sarah was lying in bed almost asleep when she realized she didn't put the garbage cans out. "Crap!" she said out loud as she threw the covers off of her and got out of bed. She threw her robe on and jammed her feet into her slippers.

It was dark in the house; she made her way down stairs and headed to the door that led to the garage. As she headed through the dark kitchen the hair on the back of her neck stood up. She turned her head towards the very dark spot in the corner of the room. Nothing.

I really need to get a grip, she grumbled. She opened up the garage door and started heading to the end of the driveway when something caught her eye again. She looked. There he was standing in his driveway watching her. It made her jump. She stopped. Looked right at him and gave him a half smile. He did nothing back, just stared. Expressionless.

Sarah was tired and cold and realized she was in her robe. *Whatever*, she shook her head and went back into her garage and shut the door. She wasn't in the mood to play his games tonight. Although she did wonder what he was doing out so late at night. She was growing more curious of him. She made her way back up to her room, this time turning on and off the lights as she passed each room.

She settled back in her bed when she saw a light come on across the way, creating a sliver of light ran across her ceiling. Curiosity got the best of her and she got back out of bed and went to her window and peeked out through the crack of the curtain. She couldn't see anything and decided then that she would go the next day and introduce herself. She went to bed. She laid there a while awake thinking about the mystery man next door. She soon drifted off to sleep.

When she woke up she was surprised, she had made it through the night with no nightmare, but she didn't feel rested at all. She got up frustrated and got ready for her day.

She tried calling the genealogist but no answer. *Hmm thought I would have heard something by now. Maybe I'll stop by while I'm out*, puzzled she put the phone down. She gathered up her things and went down stairs. She was in the kitchen when she heard a knock at her front door, making her jump. She was very jumpy these days. She went to the door and opened it. Nobody was there but an 9x12 envelope. She picked it up and looked at it. It was addressed to her but had no return address and it was heavy. She quickly walked down her walkway and looked down each way of her street. No vehicles, not even sounds of one. She let out a sigh and went back into her house. She went to the kitchen and sat down at the counter. While finishing up her must have coffee she opened the envelope. It was the folder she had given the genealogist. *What in the world*, finding a letter along with it.

Dear Ms. Guastella,

I regret to inform you but I cannot complete your request at this time. I wish you the best of luck, but unfortunately you will be on your own with this project. My advice to you, STOP looking.

Sincerely,
Craig Hansen

"*What in the world? What does that mean? STOP looking?*" she questioned getting a little upset. She picked up the phone and called Mr. Hansen. *The number you have dialed has changed or no longer in service, please try the number again...* the recorded operator's voice said. "Why is this happening again?" she exhaled as she slammed the phone down on the counter and then picked it back up to inspect it for damage. She gulped down the last of the coffee and grabbed her things including the folder and headed out.

Her first stop was to Mr. Hansen's office. She pulled up to the building to find it closed. More then closed, it was empty when she looked in the windows. She knew one thing, now more then ever; she wasn't going to stop looking. Something weird was going on and it enticed her more. What was in her family's past that was so bad that something had happened to two genealogists and told to stop? She was going to find out. She had an office now so she would just work on it herself when she had free time to do so. Sarah ran the rest of her errands and then met up with Jenny and Samantha for lunch. She filled them in on her family search and asked them what they thought.

"Sounds creepy, are you going to stop?" Samantha asked.

"She can't!" Jenny cut in.

"Are you kidding? What if there's something bad happening? What if SHE ends up getting hurt, or worse?" Samantha argued.

"But that just makes me want to know more. What is it that is so bad in my family's past?" Sarah quizzed looking down at her plate as she twirled her fork in the salad that she hardly touched. Her friends stop the debate between the two of them and looked at Sarah.

"Well I'm behind you with anything you need," Jenny answered as she tapped on Sarah's hand with hers. Samantha gave in and agreed with Jenny.

"Thank you that means a lot," Sarah said.

There was a moment of silence, when Samantha spoke, "I'm moving."

"What?" Jenny and Sarah said at the same time.

"I got a job in New York. It's a big break

for me. I'm going to be an anchor at the sister station," Samantha explained.

"That's great!" again Jenny and Sarah said together. They all laughed.

"When do you leave?" Sarah asked.

"Well that's the down side, tomorrow morning."

"What?" Jenny yelled and then covered her mouth with her hand quickly. They all laughed again. Jenny looked around the restaurant. People were staring and she could feel her cheeks getting warm. Sarah and Samantha laughed. They could count on one hand how many times they had seen Jenny get embarrassed.

Sarah was going to miss Samantha. She looked at her friends and although her friendship with Jenny was stronger, the three of them had been friends since elementary school. Jenny was the fun, balls to the wall, no guts no glory friend and Samantha was the level headed, no risk friend. Samantha had a plan for everything, she had her life mapped out since she was five and never steered away from that. Sarah envied both her friends. She fell somewhere in the middle.

"Well I decided I'm going to be brave like Jen here and go introduce myself to my dark, creepy, mystery neighbor next door" Sarah said slow and quiet, in an unsure voice.

"It's about time!" Jenny roared loudly. She saw someone looking at her from the table next to them. "WHAT?" as she made a little face.

Sarah and Samantha giggle quietly and Jenny laughed.

"Oh man, I'm going to miss the gossip!" Samantha pouted.

"Don't worry. If we have gossip we will get together and call you" Jenny interjected.

"You two better," she sassed back.

"Well I don't care how late it is, you better call me immediately after your encounter with him with all the juicy details" Jenny squawked pointing at Sarah.

"Gesssh Jenny" Samantha breathed.

"What?" Jenny laughed.

"Well I haven't done anything yet" Sarah stated.

"Yeah that we know," Jenny said sarcastically as she nudged Sarah and smiled.

"Ha ha," Sarah snickered back. Just then she got chills. She had a feeling that someone was watching her. She glanced around the restaurant and there he was sitting at a table across the room from her, watching her. She continued looking around the room as she told her friends that he was there.

"You must be losing your mind," Jenny laughing, "No one is sitting over there." Samantha nodding her head agreeing with Jenny.

"He's right...." Sarah started to say as

she turned to look over to where he was. There was nothing, but an empty chair.

"He was right there at that table!" she exclaimed.

Jenny and Samantha looked at each other with uncertainty.

"Maybe you need to take a vacation. I hear New York is nice this time of year," Samantha said smiling.

"But .." she stopped herself from speaking knowing that whatever she would say her friends would make it sound worse, "Maybe your right," she gave in. They had finished their lunch and were walking out saying their good byes when Sarah used the excuse that she left her keys on the table and went back in. Jenny and Samantha left.

Sarah went up to the waitress and asked if a man dressed in black clothing had just been sitting at the table in the corner.

"Oh you must be talking about Luke, Yes he was here. He comes in here once a week, same day, and same time; Like clock work. Doesn't say much though and when he does he is polite and a big tipper," the waitress said with a smile.

"Thank you," Sarah said satisfied that she wasn't losing her mind. *Luke huh?* She thought. She wondered if he went there because she always met her friends on that day, at that time. It has been their thing for as long as Sarah could remember. She tipped the waitress for the information and left.

She stopped by the grocery store, she knew she didn't have any food in her refrigerator and had planned on staying in for the weekend in hopes to get some research done. If she only remembered all actions have a reaction.

It was early evening before Sarah made it home. As she pulled in she looked over at Luke's house. As soon as she put her things away she would go over. She had to keep telling herself over and over that she was going to go over and introduce herself to him like the little engine that could.

She let out a sigh and walked out her door and in the direction of his. She could feel her heart beating faster as she walked up his walkway. She hesitated before knocking. She couldn't see any lights on through the white smoky tinted windows in the front door. Dark; as usual.

She thought she saw a shadow pass by the door but it didn't seem anyone was home, no lights, no sound. Silence. She would try again later. She turned to leave and saw her neighbor, Mrs. Wilson checking her mail across the street.

"Good evening Mrs. Wilson." Sarah shouted waving.

"Good evening Sarah," Mrs. Wilson replied watching Sarah walk over.

"How are you and Mr. Wilson doing?

"We are doing well. See you were over at

the neighbors. Meet him?" She inquired as she raised an eyebrow.

"No. You?"

"No. The mister and I were just saying how odd he seems to be, but he seems to have a liking to you."

"Why do you say that, Mrs. Wilson?"

"We have noticed him watching you from time to time."

"Really? hmmm." Sarah questioned, "I just tried to introduce myself, but he didn't appear to be home."

"You like him, do you?" Mrs. Wilson quizzed with a smile. Sarah couldn't help but smile back. Truth is, Sarah was becoming very drawn to him. Although something inside her told her to be scared of him.

"Well he had just come home not more then an hour ago, he must have snuck out again" Mrs. Wilson finished.

"He seems a little strange" Sarah sighed.

"Let us know if you need anything dear."

"Thank you Mrs. Wilson."

"Anytime dear."

Sarah watched as Mrs. Wilson went back into her house and then she walked back over and went inside her own home. As she shut the door she could hear the phone ringing. She got to it in time.

"Hello?" She answered the phone.

"Hey friend of mine, with Robert out of town, I have free time and I'm not feeling the stay at home thing, wanna meet for drinks? Pleeeaasseee?" Jenny pleaded.

"Sure," Sarah answered. She didn't really want to be at home either. "What time?"

"About 8pm?" Jenny answered.

"Ok sounds good, see you then."

Sarah hurried and made something to eat. She got ready and was driving out when Luke's house caught her attention. She could see light coming from behind the curtain in the upstairs window. *Figures*, she huffed as she drove by.

She met up with Jenny at their normal hang out. She was really glad to be out. She didn't want to be alone and she loved spending time with her dearest friend.

"I'm so glad you decided to come tonight," Jenny said.

"Me too," Sarah answered.

They ordered their drinks and Sarah glanced around the lounge. *It was pretty quiet for a Friday night,* she thought, but didn't mind. The crowd that was there seemed to be having a good time.

"Thank you," Jenny and Sarah said to the waiter for the drinks.

"I went over to the neighbor's house," Sarah said breaking the silence.

"Oh. Really?" Jenny inquired as she raised her eye brow.

"Yes really, but no answer. The funny thing was I could have sworn I saw something or someone pass by the door. There's little window panes in the door but not clear, anyway maybe I was seeing things. When I was leaving I saw Mrs. Wilson outside and she said that they have caught him watching me."

"Maybe he likes you, but he's shy," she said in a teasing manner.

"Maybe," Sarah said while rolling her eyes.

The drinks seem to be going down easy, too easy. Before they knew it, they were at the dance club down the street from the lounge. Jenny and Sarah were having a great time but Sarah had thought it would have been nice if Samantha would have decided to come out with them. Apparently Samantha told Jenny she was too busy getting packed up to join. Sarah wondered if this was the start of them all going in different directions. Most friends do that after high school and Sarah was grateful that they were in their late twenties and still as close as when they were in high school.

Sarah could feel herself getting tipsy but didn't care. She was going to let loose and have fun with Jenny, besides Jenny said she could crash at her place seen is how it was closer. She couldn't remember the last time she had this much to drink. It seemed to her that as soon as her drink was about empty, another one appeared in front of her. She didn't know where the drinks were coming from and figured it was Jenny doing it behind her back, although Jenny was denying it. *Definitely something she would do,* Sarah judged.

Over in the corner of the club she failed to notice that he was there watching her, that he had been watching her since she arrived at the lounge and that he was the one buying the drinks. He was becoming more and more fascinated by her, but he shouldn't; he couldn't, he was there for one reason, to end the curse. This upset him, as he watched her on the dance floor, seeing that she was clearly getting drunk. He laughed. *A few more drinks,* he thought and then he will make his move. He was mesmerized by the way she moved.

"Stop it," he kept saying to himself. But he was becoming drawn to her. At first it was because he was so focused on revenge but now he was starting to like what he saw. He had to stay focused. It could ruin everything if he didn't.

"What would the harm be in having some fun with her" he thought, until he had an opportunity to make his move. He couldn't take his eyes off of her. Just then a man danced towards Sarah showing interest in her. Instantly Luke was angry. He didn't like that strange man trying to make a move on her. *Where is this jealousy coming from,* he grimaced. Maybe it

wasn't jealousy, maybe more like rage at the thought of that guy screwing up his plans. He had to stop the guy. He got up and walked over to them on the dance floor. He hated dancing. He smiled, the guy's pick up line was horrible, but with Sarah being drunk he figured she wouldn't know the difference.

He was standing right behind her, so close. He looked dead square in the eyes of the guy and said in a stern, deep voice, "She's with me."

The wild look in Luke's eyes must have said it all because the guy backed off and tried to pick up Jenny. That didn't work either so eventually he disappeared in the crowd. Sarah was so drunk she didn't realize he was right behind her. The mysterious man next door; Luke. She was oblivious.

Chapter 6

"Oh man my head hurts," Sarah winced as she fought to open her eyes. It was bright and she could hear water being turned on in the other room. It sounded like a shower turning on. At first she thought she was at Jenny's house but the bed and room wasn't familiar. When she slowly sat up, she realized she had no clothes on and clutching the sheet to her body. *Where am I? What happened last night?* She wondered as she looked around the room noticing her clothes in a trail from the door to the bed. *Oh God what have I done? What happened to Jenny?* She questioned herself.

The room did look familiar in a way. The décor was dark but nice. There was a dresser in the corner and a small desk in another corner and of course the bed. The floor plan was not much different then hers. *How odd.* She peeked out the window, *OH MY GOD, NO WAY*! She quickly covered her mouth with her hand to prevent herself from screaming. She saw the Wilson's house across the street. She quickly gathered up her clothes and was in the process of putting them on when she looked up from the bed and saw that the closet door was slid open about two inches. Enough to have something in it catch her eye.

She got up and quietly slid the closet open more. There sat the oldest chest she had ever seen. It was so cool. Something was sticking out of the side. *What is that?* She was intrigued as she glanced over at the door. She could still hear the water running. She focused her attention back on the chest. She carefully and quietly opened the top. Her mouth dropped open again; it was the night shirt she thought she had misplaced.

"How in the hell did he get it?" she breathed. She pulled it out and continued to look through the chest, her arms were getting goose bumps, and she knew she should get out of there before she got caught but the stuff in the chest was so old. She saw an old leather bound journal and flipped through it noticing some of it was written in Italian. She then pulled out a black velvet drawstring pouch. It was heavy for such a small pouch. She opened it up and saw it was some sort of medallion. Chills ran down her back. She needed to get out of there. She quickly put it all away, even left her nightshirt in the chest the way she found it.

She closed the closet and quietly and as quick as she could went down the stairs. She got half way down when the stair creaked. She stopped dead in her tracks. Her heart was pounding hard. Water was still going. She continued to the bottom. She stopped at the front door and reached for the handle. When she remembered being on the other side of the door. Her hands were shaking.

The water stopped running. *Oh no!* Sarah couldn't leave through the front door; she didn't want her neighbors seeing. She ran to the back door, by the kitchen, looking over into the kitchen as she was opening the door and saw her purse on the counter. She grabbed it and made it back to the door when she could hear the bathroom door opening upstairs. Her entire body started shaking and she had hoped she shut the door quiet enough not to alert him. She ran across the yard to hers and made it to her back door. She didn't know what was pounding harder, her head or her heart. She fumbled with her purse as she fished out the keys.

Hurry, Hurry, her inner voice nagged as she looked over at his back door. Her door opened. Panic stricken she fell in and slammed the door behind her locking it. She checked all the windows and the front door to make sure they were locked and all curtains shut. She didn't turn anything on. She went upstairs and closed herself in her room, swiped the blanket off the foot of the bed and wrapped herself up in it and curled up on the floor in one of the corners.

It was then that Sarah realized she was still holding her purse and had the worst headache she had ever felt. She began to cry. She opened up her purse and dumped the contents on the floor in front of her. Her hands were shaking so hard she could barely pick up her cell phone, let alone dial Jenny's number.

"Pick up, please pick up," Sarah begged in a weeping voice. She heard a noise outside so she pulled herself up and walked over to the window; keeping herself wrapped tight in the blanket. She peaked through the curtain and saw his car pulling out of his garage. The car stopped half way down the driveway, paused for a minute then continued. Once it hit the street it sped away. She was relieved to see him go. It was then that she realized she was still on the phone and heard Jenny's voicemail.

"Damn" she breathed as she ended the call. "I've got to get out of here." She went into her bathroom, locked the door behind her and took a shower. She packed a few days worth of clothes and personal items figuring she would bunk with Jenny or at the very least stay at a hotel the rest of the weekend, and avoid seeing him. She felt like a paranoid wreck as she drove over to Jenny's house, always looking in her rearview mirror and over her shoulder.

Sarah must have pounded on the door several times before she heard signs of life from the other side of the door. The door slowly opened, it was Jenny. Sarah snickered; Jenny looked worse then Sarah felt. *Good not the only one hung over*, she thought.

"Sarah?" Jenny questioned with squinting eyes.

"Help," Sarah broke down sobbing.

"Sarah what's wrong?" hearing the panic in Sarah's voice as she let her in.

"What happened last night?"

Jenny thought about it for a minute and

said, "I don't know. I remember drinking and dancing with you at the club and then waking up feeling half dead in my bed with this killer headache."

Jenny walked Sarah into the living room and sat her down on the couch. Seeing that Sarah was clearly shaking, Jenny put a blanket around her.

"Would you like a cup of tea?" Jenny asked her distraught friend.

"Yes that would be nice."

Jenny returned a few minutes later with two cups of tea and handed one to Sarah.

"What happened? Why are you shaking so badly?"

"I woke up this morning and not in my bed." Sarah started crying again.

"Then where?" Jenny growing more concerned having never seen Sarah in this condition before and she has seen her go through a lot over the years.

"I woke up in my neighbor's bed."

"WHAT!?!" Jenny shrieked

"There's more"

Jenny sat there with her mouth and eyes as wide as they could get.

"I was naked and didn't know where I

was at first. My clothes were all over the bedroom floor and when I was getting dressed," Sarah sobbing, "I saw this really old chest in his closet and my night shirt was in it."

Jenny just sat there in shock. She couldn't believe what was coming out of her best friend's mouth. Sarah was the predictable, overly safe friend. *What HAD happened last night*, Jenny fretted as Sarah went on.

"He was taking a shower. I had never been so scared, so creeped out. I found my purse on his kitchen counter. Grabbed it and heard the bathroom door open."

"What did you do?" Jenny was beside herself and scared for her friend.

"I got the hell out of there as fast as I could and locked myself in my room until I heard him leave. I don't want to go back right now."

"You don't have too. You can stay here. I'll have the maid make up the spare room for you."

"Ok," Sarah said with relief.

"Ok. Is there anything you need from your house?"

"Yeah I packed some things but forgot some stuff. I was just trying to get out of there as fast as I could."

"Don't worry about it. Why don't you make a list of the things you need and I will go get them." Jenny instructed in a mother like tone.

They sat in silence for a few minutes then Jenny got up and took a shower. Sarah had the list ready by the time Jenny was ready to go.

"Stay here and lock the door behind me and get some rest," Jenny instructed.

"Ok," Sarah whispered exhausted. She hoped that Jenny was able to get her things without any problems.

Jenny pulled up to Sarah's house and kept an eye on the house next door, it was dark, no life to it and creepy. She got in without any trouble and locked the door behind her. She was able to find everything Sarah had listed and fairly quick. She didn't want to be there any longer then she had to be. She locked the door and turn to go towards her car and noticed something dark off to her right. Hair stood up on the back of her neck remembering everything that Sarah had said about her encounters with the mystery man. She turned to look but nothing was there. She felt herself moving faster to her car. She couldn't leave fast enough and kept looking in her mirrors to make sure she wasn't being followed.

Jenny felt sorry for Sarah if this is how she had been feeling and now to think she had been taken advantage of. It not only pissed Jenny off but she hurt for Sarah. Sarah has been such a dear friend since grade school. She thought of her more like a sister.

Jenny stopped by the store and got some of Sarah's favorite things and picked up some feel good chick flick movies. She was going to make it a fun girl's night in or at least try.

When Jenny returned home, Sarah was

napping on the couch and let her be. She needed some sleep and Jenny hoped that when she woke she would feel a little better.

When Sarah woke up she found magazines and movies on the coffee table and could hear Jenny in the kitchen. Sarah smiled, stretched and got up. She felt bad for falling asleep but obviously she needed it.

"Sorry I passed out. What time is it?"

"No worries Sarah. It's about 5ish."

"Oh wow, I slept the whole day away."

"Sarah, you needed it. Oh by the way, your things are in the spare room."

"Thank you so much. Were there any problems?"

"Not a one," Jenny winked as she finished cooking dinner. She wasn't going to tell her that she thought he was watching her. Sarah had been through enough.

"I picked up a couple of movies, figured we could have a girls night in," Jenny added.

"Sounds perfect," Sarah exhaled with relief. She wanted to keep a low profile the rest of the weekend. It scared her to think of how he got a hold of her night shirt. She didn't want to go back home but knew she couldn't stay at Jenny's forever and looked forward to Monday. She could bury herself in her work. At least it would keep her mind busy on other things; other then what happened.

It was an enjoyable evening. They ate dinner, which Sarah had forgotten what a great cook Jenny was. The movies were light hearted. Jenny always seemed to know what Sarah needed to feel better. They talked and laughed. Sarah was very grateful for Jenny. She was a very good friend, the best. She looked at Jenny more like family, a sister she never had. Sarah could see the guilt in Jenny's eyes when she looks at her.

"It's not your fault Jenny," Sarah consoled.

"If I didn't call you then this wouldn't have happened," Jenny retorted with hurt in her voice.

"Jenny, you didn't force me to get drunk. I did that on my own."

"I just feel so bad though."

"Please don't," Sarah said softly.

"Ok. Well enough of this talk. This is suppose to be a good night," Jenny said.

"Deal," Sarah agreed. They watched movies late into the night, laughing.

He didn't know where she had gone. He thought he had kept a close eye on her place. He had seen her friend come and go with a gym bag. *Wonder if Sarah is staying with her. Wonder if she would tell Sarah she saw me watching her,* he thought. He would just have to wait until Monday, go to her work and see where she goes from there. He had the perfect opportunity to get rid of the curse Friday night and he was mad at himself for not taking it but she was so drunk, and he wanted her to know what was coming to her. He was mad at himself for losing control and sleeping with her. Obviously that didn't quench the thirst he had for wanting to be with her. He knew she wouldn't remember what they had done; he fixed it so she wouldn't and she most likely thinks he took advantage of her. In a way he did just that. It was going to be a long couple of days.

The rest of the weekend was relatively uneventful, Sarah was happy to have Monday come. Some sense of normalcy. The day was flying by due to her heavy work load so she opted to have lunch in her office just so she could get everything finished. After lunch Mr. Davis called her into his office.

"Mr. Davis?" Sarah asked as she entered into his office.

"Ah yes, Sarah, come in. I have a project for you" he said as she sat down. "Pack your bags, your going to Italy to meet one Ms. Sophia Moretti. She has hired us to do some research on her family's past. She wants the best I have and that's you. Plus I thought I heard through the grapevine that you wanted to go back to Italy." He said with a big smile on his face knowing she couldn't turn it down.

Perfect timing, she thought. "When do I leave?"

"I know it's soon but this evening. My secretary has your itinerary and I'm not sure how long you will be there so we rented you an apartment and your ticket is open on return, and please while you're there take some time for yourself. You look like you could use a vacation." He added, "after all it is on us." He smiled, "now go get ready, enjoy!"

"Thank you Mr. Davis," Sarah was excited. She went into her office and for the first time in days she couldn't stop smiling. She called Jenny with the news. Jenny was excited for her. Sarah received the file, itinerary and her ticket from Mr. Davis's secretary and headed for home. It wasn't until she turned on to her street when she realized that her heart had started beating a little faster at the thought of running into Luke.

She pulled in to her driveway quickly and glanced over towards his lifeless and dark house. She hoped he wasn't home. She quickly packed a couple of suitcases and the file, her own file and passport. She made sure everything was off and locked. She went across the street to let the Wilsons know where she was going and asked if they would keep an eye on her house and gave them the spare key.

Mrs. Wilson walked her out and told her that Luke had come and gone a few times and watched her place and had been gone all day today. She didn't really care to know his whereabouts except to know he wasn't there at that moment. She said her goodbyes to Mrs. Wilson and pulled out. Out of habit, she looked in her rear view mirror, back at her place and saw him pull into his driveway.

"That was close," she sighed.

Chapter 7

Sarah arrived in Italy late in the evening and the first thing she did was called Jenny to let her know that she had made it. She hated long flights. Although she loved to travel, she was a bit afraid of flying.

"Have you gotten to your place yet?" Jenny asked.

"No, just landed. I haven't even gotten off the plane and from the looks of it, it will be awhile. The plane is full and of course I'm in the back."

"Yeah that sucks, but considering the project in the bigger picture, what's a little wait on the plane, right?"

"You're right."

"What? I'm right? Hmm marking that on the calendar as we speak," Jenny joked.

"Ha ha, cute Jen."

"I thought so; anyway call me when you get to the apartment. I want to know what it looks like, besides then I know your there safe."

"Ok Jen. Will do," Sarah said as she tried to hide a yawn.

"I heard that. Try and relax and get some rest too" Jenny said in a stern voice. She worried about Sarah, wondering how well she was taking care of herself. They said their goodbyes for the moment and Sarah swore she would call back once at the apartment.

The airport was huge. It had changed so much since the last time she was there. Parts were closed due to construction, which made it more difficult to find the luggage area. *Look for the signs with a picture of a bag, cant be that hard,* she told herself. She was impressed by how extremely different the airport was. After getting her things, she walked outside and was about to hail a cab when she saw a limo chauffer holding a sign with her name on it. *Sweet! Thank you Mr. Davis,* she smiled. Sarah was so tired from the travel that she fell asleep in the limo and missed the ride from the airport. She woke to the driver calling out her name.

"Oh my goodness, I apologize," Sarah said a little embarrassed. The driver just shook his head as to let her it was ok. He helped her bring up her luggage and after tipping him, he left.

She opened the door to the apartment and was in instant awe of the place. It was nothing like she had seen before. It was absolutely beautiful. For the most part it had the look of the past but with some updates, like the kitchen, new oven/stove, there was a microwave, and the couches in the living room were big oversized earth toned couches. They look so inviting to Sarah after such a long day. Pictures of the rolling vineyards and country side hung throughout. The lighting in the apartment was soft, not bright like she was use to back home. It was a nice change. She pulled back the long curtain in the living room to reveal a door to a small balcony. It was dark outside but she didn't care. She walked out and was blown away by the view. Lights were twinkling as far out as her eyes could see. *Breathtaking, can't wait to see it in the daylight,* she thought as she stood there a moment longer getting caught up in all the sparkles. Sarah went down the hall and opened the first door, the bathroom. It was fairly large. She giggled at the sight of the toilet. It was in its own little closet and at the far end of the bathroom, a stand up shower, big enough for one person and a huge claw foot tub. *Perfect, can't wait to have a nice hot, relaxing bubble bath,* she thought.

Sarah went down the hall to the last door. As she opened it she could feel her mouth drop open. A huge four poster bed dominated the room with its massive presence. It was a dark wood, *maybe cherry.* It had white and champagne color bedding and lots of pillows with white sheer drapes around the bed. Pictures in old rustic frames, like the ones in the living room hung on the walls. She had put her bags down by the closet to unpack later. She went back into the kitchen; something had caught her eye when she did a quick glance when she walked by. A huge basket of fruit, chocolates and wine sat on the counter with a card attached.

Sarah,

Enjoy the stay in Italy. I hope you find peace and relaxation amongst the work. I took the liberty to have a few things put in the cupboards and refrigerator for you. Hope you find everything to your satisfaction. I expect daily updates. Have fun and again enjoy.

Mr. Davis,

That was so thoughtful, she thought as she opened up the cupboards and the refrigerator to check out his handy work, finding herself shocked at how full they were. He had thought of everything she would need. Sarah was impressed. "I love my job," she spoke out loud smiling. She ran into the bedroom and pulled her cell phone from her purse and called Jenny back.

"You are not going to believe this place," Sarah blurted out when she heard Jenny answer the phone.

"That good huh?"

"Oh yeah. Mr. Davis thought of everything. The cupboards and fridge is stocked and this place is so beautiful, the view from the balcony is gorgeous at night that I can hardly stand it. I can't wait to see it in the daylight. Oh, and the bed, I will take lots of pictures, you would love it here."

"Wow, I'm so jealous."

"Oh and there's a huge basket with wine, and a huge claw foot tub in the bathroom!"

"You should crack open the wine and take yourself a bubble bath, then get a good nights sleep," Jenny said

"Oh I will."

"So what happens now?"

"Well, I meet with Sophia at 10 to discuss what it is she wants to know about her family's past and then I suppose I will get started on it."

"And what about exploring the sights, or working on your own family stuff?"

"Well I have been here before so I shouldn't get too lost, unless they have remodeled the whole place since I was last here," Sarah chuckled then continued, "I figured I will take the weekends for that."

"Hey! Maybe Robert will let me hop over there for a week to see you. I could lend a hand, help you?" Jenny said with question to her half statement.

"That would be so great if you could."

"I'll ask him tonight when he gets home" Jenny said with excitement. "Oh, I forgot to ask, who's watching your place? Besides creepy?"

"The Wilsons are."

"Ok, good."

"Creepy?" Sarah laughed.

"Yes. I think he was watching me when I went to get your things but when I looked over, nothing was there, but I swear someone was standing there," Jenny rattled.

"I'm sure he was. He does that and yes it is creepy. Why didn't you tell me?" Sarah was relieved to know she was thousands of miles away from him.

"You were already so upset. I didn't want to add to it," just the thought of it sent chills through Jenny again. "Well you're there now so no worrying about creepy or anything to do with him," Jenny added.

"Yes mother," Sarah boosted sarcastically. Jenny laughed.

"Ok well its late here and I'm getting off this thing and jump in that tub," Sarah yawned; exhausted from the day of travel.

"Ok, I'll call you tomorrow and let you know what Robert says."

"Alright, good night," Sarah said hanging up the phone, grabbed the basket and went into the bathroom. She put the basket down by the tub and ran a bubble bath. She poured a glass of wine and reached up above the tub and opened the window. A nice cool breeze blew in. She slowly slid herself into the hot water and laid back. *Perfect*, she thought as she picked up the glass and sipped on the wine. *Mmmmm will have to add wine tasting to the list of to-do,* she thought as she swished the wine around in the glass remembering how much fun it was last time she was in Italy.

After the relaxing tub, she put her pajamas on, grabbed the camera out of her purse and took the basket back to the kitchen. Sarah found her way back out on the balcony again and took more pictures of the night sky. Sarah decided to turn in after the picture taking. She was tired and wanted to appear to be well rested for Sophia.

When Sarah woke up, it was bright. She started to think that she over slept the alarm but she hadn't. In fact, she woke up an hour before she was suppose to and to her surprise felt good. She stretched and got out of bed, walked over to the window and peaked out. It was so bright it hurt her eyes. She went into the kitchen and made herself some breakfast and took it out to the small table on the balcony. The view was even more breathtaking then the night before. She took her time eating, breathing in the smells of the morning air. For the first time in a long time Sarah felt so relaxed, at peace.

She got ready and headed out. Sarah knew where the café was that she was meeting Sophia and because it was only a few blocks away she decided to walk and take in the beauty of the city. It was a quaint little café when she found Sophia sitting at one of the outdoor tables, at least it looked like the same woman as the one in the photo that Mr. Davis gave her.

"Sophia?" Sarah asked the dark haired, beautiful Italian woman sitting alone at the table.

"Yes" Sophia replied as she stood up taking Sarah's hand in her own.

"I'm Sarah, from Global Research. Hope I didn't keep you waiting long."

"Oh no, in fact, your early." Sophia replied with a thick accent as she motioned Sarah to take a seat across from her. Sarah complied. As soon as Sarah sat down a waiter appeared. She ordered an espresso and got down to business.

Sophia handed Sarah a folder containing all the information she had about her family's past. Sarah opened the folder and glanced through it as Sophia continued talking.

"My father died about 15 years ago and after that I had received a box from my mother and a letter saying that I was never to open it and that she would be asking for it back eventually."

"Interesting."

"Yes. Well, it gets a little more; as you say, bizarre. I had it for a few years before she asked for it back. But I had looked into it. I opened it from the bottom so my mother wouldn't know that I looked. I took pictures of the contents. There are copies of the pictures in the folder. When my Grandfather had died I had gone back to Italy and while at my grandparents I found this folder and in it contained a Global Research business card and your name written on the back."

"My name?" That puzzled Sarah.

"Yes, I assumed that you were the best at your company if my grandfather had your name written down and well, your boss confirmed it. Anyway, I have included in the folder, the research I did, which unfortunately isn't much. I do know that the items in the pictures are very old, possibly hundreds of years old. I would like to know what the meaning to all this is. What the secrecy is. I asked my mother once but given her quick response and not in a good way, I decided to find out on my own. I never knew what my father or grandfather did for a living and my father was very mean but because of our upbringing you don't question adults."

Sarah was very intrigued by what Sophia was saying and looking at the pictures of the items, she couldn't wait to get started. *Fascinating*, she thought.

"No one in my family knows I'm doing this and I would like to keep it that way. My family has been here for centuries and everybody knows our name, so please try and lay low as far as asking around. I know it's asking a lot but I would really appreciate it."

"I understand. No problem."

"Here are my numbers; where I work and my home. Call anytime you need too," Sophia said.

"I will do more then my best," Sarah said with confidence.

"Thank you. I must go before I'm seen with you and questions are asked," Sophia said.

"I'll be in touch," Sarah said as she looked down at the folder and then back up. Sophia was gone. Sarah looked down both ways of the sidewalk but Sophia was no where to be seen. *She really doesn't want to be spotted with me*. Sarah laughed at how fast Sophia disappeared.

After Sarah left the café she decided to walk around for a bit, to re-familiarize herself with the area. She found the farmers market, the courthouse and the museum. She also passed by what appeared to be an outdoor theater. *Definitively will have to come back during the weekend to see if anything is going on*, she said to herself as she put it on her mental checklist of things to do. After walking around taking a lot of pictures, Sarah realized her feet were starting to hurt and she was getting hungry.

Sarah made it back to the apartment and unpacked the rest of her things, set up her computer at the dinning room table and gathered all the information she had received and put them next to the computer. She made a sandwich and grabbed water out of the refrigerator and went out on the balcony; her new favorite place. It was a warm sunny day. Like at breakfast, she ate slow enjoying all the sights and sounds.

"Ok let's see what I've gotten myself into." She sighed out loud as she sat down at the table. She opened up the folder to see what Sophia had accomplished. Like Sophia said, not much. She went on the internet and started searching Sophia's family's past. She needed to complete the family tree first and as for the items in the pictures, if Sophia is right and they are hundreds of years old, then she may need help. Unfortunately, the internet isn't always that helpful, which amused her. She would have to check out the library and maybe the museum.

She wondered if anyone had poster board or something close to that here. It would help create a visual time line and family tree. She thought about getting enough to do her own family findings as well. Sarah made a list of things she would need. It was late afternoon and still very warm out so Sarah decided to walk again. She went into a few little shops but they didn't have anything even close to what she was looking for. As she was passing by an art gallery, she decided to try there. She figured if they didn't have what she was looking for that they could point her in the right direction. The art work was beautiful. Some of the most exquisite she had ever seen. Sarah didn't speak fluent Italian but enough to get by. The lady at the desk, at the front of the gallery, told her to go down two blocks, take a right, then down about three more. Wouldn't be hard to find the lady had said.

She took a lot of pictures a long the way. She found the little shop the lady told her about. She was surprised to see that it carried more then what she thought it would. She found poster board, colored markers, post-it notes, pocket notebook, a few regular sized notebooks and a photo album. She ended up with more then she went in there wanting and had to hail a cab for the ride back to the apartment.

With full hands, she managed to get into the apartment and dropped the bags by the table. She picked just the poster board up and took it to the bedroom. The only room with enough wall space to work with. She took down two photos and stuck them on the shelf in the closet, then hung the poster board up, half on one wall and half on the other wall. She labeled one Sophia's tree and the other one Sarah's tree. Sarah went to the table and grabbed the folder and the color markers and went back into the bedroom. She started drawing out Sophia's tree but didn't get very far; it stopped with her great- great grandfather. *Hmm, got my work cut out for me,* she said to herself. She put the folder on the bed and walked over to her own tree and did what she could there. But again she didn't get very far. Frustrated she picked up the folder and walked back into the living room, tossing the folder on the table as she passed it.

She noticed the time and remembered that she still needed to write an email to Mr. Davis. *Better do it know while I'm thinking about it,* she sighed.

Mr. Davis,
Thank you so much for the beautiful apartment and everything in it. The basket was very thoughtful as well and I enjoyed the wine. I met with Ms. Moretti this morning and have already begun on her search. I have taken pictures of the town and will email them as soon as I get them downloaded. Thank you again and I will write again tomorrow.
Sincerely,
Sarah

Her cell phone rang, making her jump.

"Hello?" She answered.

"Hey, it's me." Jenny said.

"So what did Robert say?" Sarah already knew why Jenny was calling. It made her smile at the thought of knowing her friend that well.

"He said yes of course!" Jenny practically yelled.

"Alright! When are you coming?"

"I leave next week and he said I could stay two weeks!!" Jenny said bursting with excitement.

"Really?" Sarah was very happy at the news. It will be nice to venture out with someone and couldn't have asked for someone better.

"Yes isn't that wonderful."

"Yes. But there's one thing; there's only one bed but the couch folds into a queen size bed. I can't wait until you get here."

"Oh don't fret Sarah, it will be fine."

"Ok, ok. So anything happening over there?" Sarah asked.

"Nope, very quiet on the home front," Jenny answered.

"Good. I need to call and check in with the Wilsons."

"Why don't I do that? It will save you on the cell bill"

"Would you? That would be great. Thank you."

"Yes. I'll go over tomorrow," Jenny said.

"That sounds good to me."

"How's it going over there?" Jenny asked.

"It's fabulous," Sarah said rubbing it in.

"I can't wait. I'm so excited. I've already gone shopping for some cute clothes to wear and I'm already half packed," Jenny said snickering.

"Your crazy," Sarah said laughing, "well let's see how much I can get done by the time you get here."

"Yeah, because I wanna go play a little while I'm there" Jenny said in a funny matter of fact voice.

"I know," Sarah laughed.

"Ok well I better go and get dinner started for Robert. I'll call you tomorrow after I talk with the Wilsons."

"Ok Jen."

They said their goodbyes and hung up. Sarah went over to the balcony and looked out. She couldn't get over how stunning the view was.

Sarah wondered if the library was opened. She grabbed her camera and notebook and headed out. She remembered seeing the library on her walk from earlier and found it without to much trouble.

According to the sign on the door, Sarah still had a couple of hours before it closed. *It's a start*, she thought as she pulled the big heavy door open. The library building was very cool, tall pillars throughout, cathedral ceilings with paintings. It was huge inside and apparent that it was very old, although she could plainly see where attempts of restoration had been done.

Sarah found a computer and looked up the Moretti family name. She was hoping it wasn't common, that would make it a more daunting task to get the information she was after, but was pleasantly surprised that she was able to track down another set of grandparents and background on the two of them. She printed it all out and put a quick reference in her notebook. She then started on the pictures of the old items Sophia had. She had the librarian scan the photos onto the computer and then Sarah did a search on every search engine the internet had. The return was very little. She printed out the pages and decided to read through them when she got back to the apartment.

She must have had around fifty pages printed out when she realized she hadn't even started looking through the books she had pulled off the shelves and the library was getting ready to close. She checked out the books, gathered up her things and headed out. It was getting late in the evening so she decided to stop at the café down the street from the apartment.

The waiter sat her at a small table against the wall and when she looked around the café she noticed that she was the only one who was by themselves. Seeing some of the people looking at her with sad eyes, she was glad to know that Jenny would be with her next week. She ate her food in peace and then made her way back to the apartment and put the papers down on the table. She will later wish that she had paid closer attention to those papers.

The rest of the week went pretty much the same. She made trips to the library and brought back more print outs of the research she found. The dinning room table was almost completely covered by weeks end. Two more days until Jenny would be joining her and Sarah was getting excited at the idea of having company. Sarah would work through the weekend by going through some of the papers and start weeding out the trash, keeping the useful stuff.

She wanted to go to the museum to see if they had anything on the items in the photos. This was by far the most interesting research job she had been assigned. She was very thankful that Mr. Davis thought so high of her work. She felt pleased with herself that she was able to clear off half of the table by the end of the night. *That deserved a glass of wine, or two,* she thought as she giggled.

Chapter 8

She arrived at the museum around 10 am hoping that it was a good time to go on a Saturday. After taking pictures of the outside she went in. She loved the architecture of the buildings in Italy. Only a few days into the trip and already had a few hundred photos. She didn't care. The inside of the museum was incredible. She could spend all day in there, like the library.

She must have seemed out of place because a woman walked up and asked if she could help. Sarah asked if there was a historian on staff that she could talk to.

"Uno memento," she said and walked away. Sarah continued to look at all the things around her.

"Ma'am, can I help you?" a man's voice said from behind her, startling her.

"Yes hopefully," Sarah said seeming doubtful as she dug out the photos from her bag. "I'm Sarah and I work for a research company in the U.S. and have these pictures of some items that were passed down through the generations of my client and she would like to know about these things. They appear to be very old and was wondering if you could help?" Sarah explained.

"Well my name is Frank. May I see?" He asked as he held out his hand toward the pictures. Sarah handed him the photos.

"I see what you mean about the items being old. I'm guessing hundreds of years old. If your client still has them I would be quite impressed by that, considering how far down the generations it would have to be passed through and not get lost," he exclaimed.

"Yes it is quite impressive," She added.

"Do you mind if I take these photos?"

"No. I have copies."

"Ok good. Give me a few days and I'll see what I can come up with," Frank said.

"That sounds good. I actually have company coming in so u can have a couple weeks if that's better?"

"Perfect," Frank said with a smile and eager to start. Sarah took note at how his eyes seem to sparkle when he saw the photos.

They swapped business cards as Sarah told him where she was staying if anything came up, thanked him for his time and left. She hoped that Frank would be able to give her some information. She looked at her watch, excited that it was still early and decided to go back to the apartment, gathered some things, shoved them in her backpack and used the rest of the day for herself.

She took out her camera and put it around her neck and started walking. She was amazed at how she could find more pictures to take of buildings she already took pictures of as if looking at them for the very first time. She asked people walking by where they thought were the best wineries and cafés for when Jenny came and at times having conversations about the town and their lives there. Sarah popped into the small shops just to see what was in them. She figured she would be there long enough, might as well see what's around her. She found another quaint little café on the outskirts of town. It too had an outdoor patio like all the others. She took a seat and ordered an espresso. *Gonna have to go to espresso rehab when I get home,* she laughed to herself. Only Jenny would have found her dry humor funny.

She was enjoying the view and espresso when someone walked up from behind her and sat down at her table making her jump.

"Sorry I didn't mean to startle you." It was Sophia.

"Oh goodness, it's ok. I seem to be jumpy more often then not" Sarah reassured her.

"I saw you sitting here so I thought I would sit a quick minute to see how things were coming along. I know it's only been a week."

"I actually have gotten a good start on it and currently waiting to hear back from a historian from the museum about the things in the photos," Sarah said.

"Oh. That's great, but did you by chance say my name?" Sophia questioned.

"No. Just said my client," Sarah reassured her.

"Ok. Good," Sophia looked relieved.

"Is there something you're not telling me?" Sarah pressed.

"No. I've told you everything. It's just the way people seem when I bring it up. Like there is some big secret in my family and I don't know if that's good or bad. Just being cautious," Sophia said. Sarah understood about being cautious as she had a flash of Luke. Goosebumps formed on her arms. Sophia looked at her watch and quickly got up, said stay in touch and left.

It was as if she appeared out of thin air and left the same way. Not at all creepy, Sarah thought sarcastically. She shook her head and smiled. Sarah finished up with her espresso and headed out. She passed by a bike rental place and stopped. *Why not.* She went in, rented a bike and off she went. She rode for miles, taking in the country side.

Something caught her eye. An old castle; and as she got closer it started to have a creepy appeal to it. It looked dark. It reminded her of the dark house next to hers, chills ran down her back. She stopped at the massive wrought iron gate. She sat on the bike, hands wrapped around the thick iron rods, mesmerized by the castle. It made the gate look small in comparison. It had what could be two look out towers and walls built from large stone bricks to keep out unwanted intruders. *It must be centuries old.* The landscaping was no different. Large thick trees lined the gate for more privacy and thick ivy covered the sides of the castle walls. The yard was dark green and the grass was thick. There were a few flower beds in Sarah's line of sight, she wondered if there were more. Other then the neatly manicured lawn and flower beds there were no other sign of life. *That seemed familiar,* she thought of Luke's house again. She started taking pictures of the castle and as creepy as it looked, she wondered what it looked like on the inside and how it looked back when it was first built. She could imagine women dressed in the corset tight dresses and the men in their suits. She chuckled at the Hollywood image she had in her head. She must have taken fifty pictures before she decided to continue on.

The butler, of the castle, Salvator saw her on the surveillance cameras. His eyes widened. *No way, that can't be her, Damien must know at once,* he hissed. He went into the study and filled Damien in on what he saw.

"Are you sure?" Damien snarled.

"Yes sir. I zoomed in and compared the pictures. It's a match. A perfect match," the faithful butler Salvator said excitedly at what he saw.

"What is she doing here?" Damien wondered. "Where is Luke?" He asked his butler, knowing he didn't know.

"I can call and find out sir," Salvator quickly replied.

"You do that."

"Right away sir," Salvator excused himself and left the study, leaving Damien deep in thought.

Sarah enjoyed the sights and sounds of the country side, and she had never felt so relaxed. She couldn't wait to take Jenny on this same route. It was an endless scene of rolling hills of grapevines and occasionally a farm house.

"Hello," Luke answered his cell phone.

"Mister Luke, Where are you?" the voice was very familiar to Luke, it was Damien's butler.

"I'm in the U.S." why was he calling, Luke wondered as he answered Salvator's question.

"Master Damien wanted me to find you and tell you that she is here, in Italy. I saw her outside the castle's gate riding a bike." There was silence.

"Mister Luke?"

"Sorry. I'm on my way." Luke said abruptly hanging up on Salvator. *Why was she in Italy?* He wondered as he heard a car drive up outside. He looked out the window and watched as Sarah's friend pulled in across the street. She talked for some time with the nosy Wilson couple and then started to leave. He quickly went to his car. He needed answers and knew he would get them from her.

He waited until she drove off and then pulled out. He followed her to her house. He watched her go in then got out and went up to the house for a better look, while keeping an eye on his surroundings to make sure no one saw him sneaking around. He picked a window that had big bushes in front of it. *Perfect,* he thought. He peaked in and could see her shadow moving around. He saw her go through what appeared to be a living room or sitting room. She had a suitcase in her hand. *She's leaving. Wonder to where?* He waited. He heard the front door open and then close. He ducked behind the bush and waited until he heard the car leave then ran to his. He could see it up ahead. *I could catch up to her no problem*, he thought as he revved up the engine.

He followed her to the store and then to the airport. He parked a few cars away from her and followed her in. She was going to Italy. *So Sarah is there, but why?* He wondered how strange it was that for all the places to vacation that those two chose not only his country, but his hometown. He watched Sarah's friend until she went through the gate for passengers only. She kept looking around, that made him laugh. He went up to the counter that she was just at and got himself his own ticket, first class of course. The lady at the counter was oozing with hormones; being overly flirtatious with him. He was amused by that. Seen is how he was already checked in and didn't want to wait a hour and a half before boarding, he decided to run back to his house and get a few things, like his passport for one. He made it back in plenty of time to catch his flight. He settled into his seat, thankful that it was going to be a long flight. He wasn't prepared to go back to Italy so soon, not like this. The only plus side, was her. He would be able to see Sarah again. He just wanted to get all this over with. This was perfect. Her death could be blamed on a vacation accident and people in the States wouldn't know any thing different. The plane took off and Luke closed his eyes.

The weekend went by quicker then Sarah thought it would. She had gotten a great start to the research and glad it was time for Jenny's visit. It was early Monday morning and Sarah was at the airport an hour before she had to be. She was to excited to sleep. Jenny's flight was delayed a couple of hours. *That figures*, Sarah thought. Sarah started getting a little tired so she decided to go to the espresso bar in the airport. One thing about where she was, there was no shortage of espresso. Had she stayed by the gate Jenny was going to come through, had her plane not been delayed, then Sarah would have seen Luke come through the gate next to the one Sarah was standing by. His plane was on time.

Luke got his luggage and headed towards home. He dreaded being here with nothing changed. He could hear his mother already. He was about half way home when he changed his mind and had the cab driver take him into town. He decided to stay at his apartment instead. His family didn't know he had it. *What they don't know won't hurt them,* he figured. Besides as far as his family was concerned, he was still in the United States, at least he had hoped.

He got settled into his apartment, it had

been a long time since he was last there. After he had finished unpacking, he decided he had better go out to the castle and see Damien before he came looking for him. He had hoped it wasn't Sarah that Salvator had seen but after watching her friend leave on a flight to Italy, he knew it was. He hated having to deal with Damien. He grabbed the keys to his car and headed out.

Luke didn't mind the castle, he thought it was pretty cool and he bet that there were a lot of stories to tell if the walls could talk. He had wished his grandmother was still alive. He had become very close to her after the summer his father died. She was the one person he could count on. She would have known how to handle this situation. He didn't trust Damien and Salvator. He knew they were very bad men. He wondered on his drive there what all Damien knew. He hated his life; the one person he was to hate and get rid of is now the one person he can't stand to be away from and this was the longest stretch that he has been away from her and it was driving him crazy. He needed a fix and bad.

As he pulled into the long driveway of the castle, his grip tightened around the steering wheel. He felt anger growing in him. He wanted to turn the car around, but he knew it was too late. He knew them well enough to know that they knew he was coming. Luke may be able to hide from his family, but not from those two evil men.

As Luke walked up to the door, it opened as if it was expecting him. He walked in slowly, just as he remembered it, dark, poorly lit, drafty, eerie and creepy. He looked around but didn't see Salvator. *Odd, he is always at the door.* He didn't bother shutting it; he knew it would close without his help. A gift of being who they were, *or a curse*, he thought. He slowly walked down the hall towards the study. He could hear whispering and as he entered the room Damien and Salvator stopped talking with each other. Salvator straightened up to a standing position and motioned for Luke to sit down. Luke complied. *Keep your cool and thoughts evil,* Luke thought to himself as he took a seat. He didn't know the extent of Damien's abilities and he couldn't chance getting caught. He was unsure of his feelings and questioned the whole curse thing. Luke was the only one to spend as much time as he had at the castle. He paid attention to everything and read books that no one else had.

He wondered if it wasn't just Damien being evil and hateful. *He seemed to hate everyone, even Salvator at times, but for some unknown reason had taken a liking to me,* Luke thought as he studied Damien's face.

"Leave us," Damien ordered Salvator waving him off.

"As you wish Master Damien," Salvator said smugly looking at Luke as he walked by, leaving the room. Luke gave him a smile knowing it would irritate Salvator more. Salvator walked down the hall and into the parlor and then through another door. One thing Salvator loved about the castle, all the secret passage ways. He ended up behind the wall to the study where Luke and Damien were. He didn't like being left out of the conversations. He would be included one way or another.

"Luke its been a while, where have you been?" Damien asked inquisitively.

"Trying to get established so that I can handle business," Luke answered without changing his tone. He tried to keep emotions out of his voice so that Damien wouldn't become suspicious.

"Why has it taken so long?" Damien growled.

"She's never home for long."

"Not good enough! She sleeps doesn't she?"

"Yes sir."

"Then take care of it Luke," Damien said harshly.

"You have been watching her for years now, end it boy!" Damien said with anger growing in his voice.

"I will."

"Now! Don't make me wait much longer or I'll take my anger out on you as well!" Damien growled as he hit his fist on the arm of the chair. Salvator started to smile. He didn't care for Luke and hated that he had to be respectful to the twit.

"Yes sir," Luke answered quietly. He only answered as little as he had to. Damien sat there watching Luke, waiting to see any difference in his demeanor, but Luke knew that, so he sat there cold as ice, like a statue.

"Don't forget who you are," Damien said in his low raspy growl.

"Not like I could even if I wanted too," Luke mumbled.

"Are you testing me boy?"

"No sir"

"What's wrong with you boy?" Damien barked.

"Nothing."

"Hmmm," Damien was growing suspicious, "go now and finished it!"

"Yes sir." Luke didn't have to be told twice, he got up and left quickly.

"I'll be watching you," Damien said as Luke was going through the door.

That's what I'm afraid of, Luke thought as he made his way down the hall towards the door. Just as he started to pass the entry way to the parlor Salvator stepped out.

"Everything go ok Mr. Luke?" Salvator inquired slyly.

Luke shot Salvator a glare as he walked out the front door, leaving Salvator standing there smiling. *What was that, so creepy, would love to smack that smile off of his face,* Luke glared as he got back into his sports car and sped out.

There she was. Jenny looks tired, but it sure is good to see her, Sarah thought. They hugged at the sight of each other. They must have looked like school aged girls. Laughing and hugging. It had only been a short time but they missed each other. After Samantha moved to New York she stopped calling Sarah and Jenny so much. Sarah and Jenny's bond grew tighter then ever. They made it back to the apartment and Jenny settled in. They were both exhausted by the lack of sleep and decided to nap, it would do them both good.

When they woke it was late afternoon, and very warm out. Sarah took Jenny to what had become her favorite café and ordered espressos and biscotti.

"I stopped by the Wilson's and filled them in on how you were doing and asked how things had been at your place," Jenny said.

"And?"

"Mrs. Wilson said that they had seen creepy come and go a lot, maybe trying to figure out where you went," Jenny said in a teasing manner, laughing.

"Well I hope he didn't see you," Sarah said.

"I know. I hurried out of there." Jenny responded as she looked around taking in the beautiful scenery and the smells of freshly baked goods in the air. Sarah looked at her friend and wondered if she looked that way the first time she had come there.

They finished their espresso and started to walk around the town. Sarah showed Jenny some sights and it seemed Jenny was taking just as many pictures as Sarah had been. That made Sarah chuckle.

"What?" Jenny asked.

"Nothing, you camera clicking tourist," Sarah said laughing. Jenny punched her in the arm.

"Ouch," Sarah yelled out, laughing harder. It made Jenny laugh too.

"Punk," Jenny said giggling. They stopped by a winery on the opposite side of town. An area Sarah hadn't ventured out to yet. It was on the list she had created from talking to the locals. They were happy with the decision to go. They sampled some of the wines and bought a couple of bottles for Jenny's stay.

That night they made dinner and sat out on the balcony. It was still very warm out and Jenny was just as in love with the view as Sarah had become.

"It's so incredible. I can see why you have been going on and on about it in your emails. Breathtaking," Jenny said in an excited child like way. It made Sarah smile to see her friend respond like that.

"There's this pub down the street I thought we could check out after dinner. I found in on the second night here. It's actually quite perfect for us really, our kind of place. If your up for it that is."

"Sounds good to me, you know me, never turn down an offer to go out, me being the social butterfly and all." Jenny said as she raised her arms trying to mimic a butterflies wing motions. Sarah laughed at her goofy friend.

"Social butterfly?" Sarah teased. Jenny giggled.

After the day Luke had at the castle he was glad he was back at his apartment. He sat on his balcony sipping his drink thinking of Sarah and thinking about the conversation with Damien. Damien had made it clear on how he felt about Sarah and upset at how long it has taken Luke to do what he needed to do. Damien gave him until the end of the month to take care of her otherwise he was going to handle it himself. *How am I going to find her?* He was feeling restless and decided to go to the little pub down the street.

The pub was crowded. He let the door close behind him as he looked around for a place to sit. He had forgotten how different Italy was in comparison to the U.S. Italians are very social people and it didn't matter if there was work the next day. They worked to live not lived to work. Luke had been to many countries and Italians by far were the most social. He found a table in the back corner of the pub. He wasn't a social person. His upbringing prevented him from having a normal childhood and the social skills needed now. He often wondered how different his life would have been if he wasn't cursed, but then again he didn't mind being a loner; so-to-speak.

Sarah and Jenny walked into the pub down the street from the apartment and were amazed at how packed it was. Not a table left and no where to stand. Everybody seemed to be enjoying themselves none the less. It was too packed for Sarah and Jenny's liking.

"Sorry Jenny. I didn't realize how packed it would be."

"It's ok, wanna try somewhere else?"

"Sure, there's another pub about two blocks away."

"Sounds good to me, it's a beautiful night."

They headed out and it only took a few minutes. They looked at each other as they opened the door as if to say here goes nothing. Although it was also packed, they did spot a couple of empty bar stools, so they walked up to the bar and sat down. The people around them were having a good time and introduced themselves. They made Sarah and Jenny feel like they belonged.

Luke wasn't feeling the pub scene after all. He couldn't stop thinking of Sarah and he was getting frustrated. He had a few drinks and decided it was time to go. He stood up to leave when a burst of laughter came from the bar and he looked over. He took a breath in, *Oh my god, she's here. Sarah*, he thought as he sat back down in his seat. She was sitting at the bar with her friend. He wondered how long they had been there. He ordered another drink. His eyes glued to her.

As Luke watched Sarah and her friend, more then hatred passed through his body. He thought that the one night stand with her would have gotten the feelings of wanting her out of his head and the next morning the way she just up and left, well that just pissed him off. So he focused on the anger but seeing her brought back that feeling of wanting her again. He had to get rid of this curse. He had to answer to Damien and his family. As much as he tried to push it away he knew he was drawn to her and he knew that was dangerous for the both of them. If Damien found out, he would surely see to it that Sarah died. He felt so confused.

He played with the idea of just disappearing but he knew that Damien would find him. It always creeped him out the way he seemed to be able to do that. He ordered drink after drink and the more he thought about the situation he was in the more upset he became and the faster the drinks went down.

He tried but couldn't keep his eyes off of her and now it's even worse knowing how she felt, how good her skin felt, how good she smelled. Every part of his body wanted her. He watched her get up and head towards the bathroom. He followed her. She looked like she has had a few drinks herself. He was mad. She was going to get it tonight. He was mad that she had such a hold on him. It wasn't suppose to happen like this and yet he couldn't shake being so drawn to her. *Why couldn't life be simple?* He thought. The bathroom was full, he could hear many voices. He waited but she ended up coming out and he had to turn around fast so she wouldn't see his face. She walked right by him and back to her stool. *She didn't even notice*, he snickered to himself.

Something was wrong, her friend's face changed, she stopped smiling and they put their coats on. *Maybe she did see me.* He followed them from a distance. They were walking at a faster pace then normal. He wondered what was going on. The women walked into a building. He paused around the corner for a couple of minutes and then walked up to the building to get a closer look. It was an apartment building.

He went in and walked up to the elevator. No that would take to long. *Figures, it wasn't the kind that showed what floor it was going to.* He hurried to the stairwell. He ran up to the second floor and looked down the hallway. No signs or sounds. He ran up to the third floor and when he opened the door he could faintly hear a woman's voice asking someone how they were feeling. The other person responded. He knew the voice. It was Sarah's voice. He peaked around the corner and saw Jenny walking into an apartment. He quickly walked up to where the door was as the door shut. He looked at the number on the door as he walked by. *So Sarah didn't feel good huh*, he thought to himself. *Did she have too much to drink?* He laughed at the thought of that. He went back outside and looked up about where her apartment was. He would come back later when he had a clearer frame of mind. He hailed a cab and was off to his flat to sleep of the alcohol.

Jenny was drawing the curtains to the living room and noticed a man getting into a cab. It gave her the chills. *No way*, she gasped, *couldn't be him, must have had more then I thought.* She was becoming as paranoid as Sarah. She felt sorry for Sarah but this trip was doing her some good. Sarah came out of her room wearing her pajamas and went into the kitchen.

"Would you like a cup of tea, hot chocolate, anything?" she asked Jenny.

"Tea sounds perfect. Would you like to watch a movie?" Jenny asked.

"Sure," Sarah responded.

By the time Sarah came into the living room with the tea, Jenny had the movie started.

"Feeling any better?" Jenny asked.

"A lot better, that was weird, it hit all of a sudden."

"Maybe it was the alcohol"

"Could have been, we did have quite a bit," Sarah said with a snicker.

"Even though that happened I had a lot of fun today," Jenny said with a smile.

"Me too, I thought we would rent bikes and take a ride out to the country side. I did it a couple of days ago and it was wonderful," Sarah said.
"Sounds great."

They watched the movie in silence and then turned in for the night.

Sarah's eyes opened and it was still dark. *No, not now*, she thought. She looked at the foot of her bed, nothing. She looked to the side of the bed and there stood a dark shadow. *No, no, no.* The shadow moved closer to her and bent down. *This couldn't be, I MUST be dreaming; My neighbor?*

"What are you doing here?" She said, knowing she was dreaming. He of course didn't respond. She knew she was drawn to him but he made her feel uneasy as well. Obviously she had to be attracted to him to be dreaming of him like this. He leaned over and kissed her forehead. She looked up at him and he kissed her cheek. She closed her eyes as she turned her head towards him and he kissed her lips. She felt chills go throughout her entire body as it heated up. She had never felt like this before. She liked this dream very much. *What did this mean?* She wondered. *Oh don't over analyze this, not right now. Enjoy it stupid,* her inner voice was yelling.

His lips were soft and passionate. She felt his hand glide down the side of her body. Her body felt like it was going to explode. The heat was so intense. His hands were strong, but gentle. Slowly his body moved on top of hers. She ran her hands down his back. It didn't feel like an ounce of fat was on him. His body felt rock hard. She smiled. She could feel something else becoming hard. He pulled his lips away from hers and kissed her other cheek and then trailed down to her neck. She didn't want this dream to end. She turned her head to the side as he continued to move down her body. No, she definitely didn't want this to end.

Chapter 9

Something was very bright behind her eye lids. She opened her eyes to a squint. It was so bright she couldn't open them up all the way. She looked around her room, nothing. *What was I expecting? The dream had to be real? Get a grip Sarah*, her inner voice was saying. She wished it would shut up. She was more then drawn to him and last nights dream just proved that. At that moment, she felt horrible for running out on him the way she did, but he still gave her the creeps too. She was so confused.

She debated on whether to tell Jenny about her dream or not. She didn't. She still felt queasy, *maybe after something to eat I will feel better*, she thought. She went into the kitchen to find Jenny already up and sitting on the balcony. It was already warm, *it's going to be a hot one, I better bring a couple bottles of water,* she said to herself. She got a piece of toast and a cup of hot tea and joined Jenny out on the balcony.

"So, ready for that bike ride today?" Sarah asked.
"Absolutely," Jenny said with a big grin.

"Good. .I know this café outside of town that we can stop and have lunch at."

"Sounds good."

They walked to where Sarah had rented the bike before. The elderly gentleman remembered Sarah and he was very happy to see her again. He had told her that she was the most beautiful American he had ever seen. It had made her blush until he used the same line on Jenny making her laugh.

"If I was only younger, you would be in trouble," he said to her. Sarah laughed harder.

They rented two bikes and set out. Jenny was in awe of the scenery, making Sarah stop every so often to take pictures. Sarah couldn't wait until Jenny saw the castle. They were almost there. Sarah didn't tell her it was there. She knew Jenny would be so excited when she saw it. They came around the corner and she kept an eye on Jenny's expressions. Sarah was not disappointed.

"OH WOW! That's so cool!" Jenny yelled out.

"Just wait until we get closer."

Jenny couldn't stop looking at the castle as it got closer and almost crashed into a bush on the side of the road. It made Sarah laugh and in turn Jenny joined her friend, laughing even louder. They stopped at the big wrought iron gate and looked down the very long driveway at the castle. Jenny took a lot of pictures, as Sarah had suspected she would do.

"It's kind of creepy," Jenny pointed out.

"That's what I thought, but it's still so cool."

"That it is."

They sat there for a few minutes studying the castle. It was mesmerizing. Sarah was drawn to it but didn't know why. She looked down at her watch and saw the time *No wonder I am getting hungry*, she thought.

"Want to go get a bite to eat?" Sarah asked. They started peddling the bikes away from the gate.

"Yes I'm starved."

They arrived at the café and saw that there was only one table left.

"Got here just in time," Sarah commented as Jenny took a look around.

"I just love how quaint and cozy all the café's are here," Jenny said.

"It's so peaceful here. It will be hard to go home," Sarah acknowledged.

"I understand that. If I wasn't married I would stay," Jenny said smiling. That made Sarah chuckle.

She knew Jenny well enough to know she would, and would bug Sarah until she did too. They had finished lunch and were sitting, enjoying the ambiance when they had a visitor.

Sophia. This shocked Sarah given Jenny being there.

"Ma'am, I think this fell out of your bag." Sophia said to Sarah. *Clever*, Sarah thought.

"Oh, thank you." Sarah said and put the envelope into her bag.

"Anytime, enjoy your day ladies," and with that Sophia disappeared in the crowd inside the café.

"That was nice and a little weird," Jenny said watching Sophia disappearing. Sarah brushed that off and changed the subject.

"There's a vineyard down the road. Wanna go?" Sarah asked.

"Sounds like fun," Jenny responded.

They rode over to the winery and took a tour through the vineyard. They even got to try their hand, or feet rather, at stomping grapes.

Luke had gone over first thing in the morning but there was no sign of Sarah and her friend. He became instantly upset. Last night was incredible. He didn't know why he did that. It was confusing him even more. He's becoming to close to her.

His cell rang.

"She is here again and someone was with her this time," the familiar voice barked.

"How long ago?"

"Ten minutes, maybe longer."

"What direction did they go?"

"West."

He hung up the phone and headed towards the castle. His phone rang again. He looked at the number, his mother, he ignored the call. *Can't deal with that right now*, he huffed. He knew he needed to keep better tabs on Sarah otherwise Damien would take matters into his own hands and he couldn't have that. The thought of him getting his hands on her made his heart race. He had to figure out what he was going to do and fast.

Before he knew it he was flying by the castle, sure that they saw him on camera. The speed would have given him away, that and the fact that he always drives fast sporty black cars. He drove for some time, passing a vineyard and an old farm house. There wasn't anything past the farm house so he turned around and started heading back towards the castle. He pulled into the winery and looked around. He saw two bicycles leaned up against the side of the building. *They must be in there*. He parked the car in a way that they wouldn't be able to see him when they came out but in a way he could still see them.

It was quite a while before they came out. *She looks so good*, he thought, *Radiant even*. He wanted her bad. He wanted this bloody curse gone too. He was becoming more and more torn. He knew if he talked to Damien he would take it into his own hands and that could mean death to both of them. He needed to stay focused. His cell rang again. It was his mother again. He answered the phone.

"Hello mother," he answered in irritation.

"Son why haven't I heard from you?" she demanded.

"Been busy," he responded in a cold tone. He didn't mean to sound harsh but he just didn't want to have the conversation he knew his mother wanted.

Sensing her son's tone she decided now wasn't a good time and kept the conversation short, "Ok, just wanted to see how you were doing."

"I'm fine."

"Ah, ok. Well call me back when you have time," she said softly.

"Ok gotta go," he could hear his mother saying something as he hung up. *Ooppss*, he breathed sarcastically.

He figured enough time had passed and it was safe to leave the parking lot. They were further then he thought they would be. He hurried by them and kept an eye on her through his rear view mirror.

A black car went racing by Sarah and Jenny.

"Stupid driver," Jenny yelled as Sarah agreed.

"Most people slow down not speed up," Jenny still ranting. That got Jenny going and Sarah was nodding her head smiling. Jenny made her laugh.

They took their time riding back. It was such a beautiful day and Sarah didn't have anything planned for them. She figured they would play it by ear. Jenny seemed to be enjoying the moment.

They made it back to the bicycle shop and turned the bikes in and then decided to go in and out of the shops along the way back to Sarah's apartment. Jenny noticed a car that looked a lot like the one that passed them so rudely. She pointed it out to Sarah. They could see an outline of someone in the car. They decided to get a closer look and as they were about the cross the street it took off. Sarah and Jenny looked at each other.

"That was strange," Sarah said.

"You're still way too jumpy," Jenny said. Sarah figured it was someone who was just stopping at one of the shops and left in a hurry, maybe late to get somewhere.

That was close, he thought as he re-parked his car so he could still keep an eye on the women. *That friend of hers needs to go home*, he said to himself. He wondered how long she would be there.

The next few days would be the same; he followed them to the stores, the markets, to another winery and the local pubs. He wanted to pay a visit to her but he couldn't. He couldn't risk it. For now, she thought of his visits as only dreams or nightmares and that's all she needed to think of them as. He also needed to stay focused.

Before they knew it a week was gone. Time was flying. Sarah knew she needed to get going on her research and didn't really want Jenny to get involved. Sophia seemed to be worried about whatever was in her family's past and if it was anything bad, stereotyping that all Italians are connected to the MOB, she would rather be the only one involved.

Chapter 10

The two weeks went very quick and in a blink of an eye, Jenny was gone. Sarah will miss her being there but glad she was gone. She had to get her work done. She only had a few weeks left besides she was sure Sophia was wondering what was going on.

She needed to go back to the museum. She figured a couple of weeks would be long enough to find something out. She thought it was strange that she hadn't heard from Frank; the historian. Maybe he had hit a dead end as well.

It was almost to hot outside and she wondered if she should walk to the museum or catch a cab. In a few weeks she would be back in the states were the summers were unpredictable so she figured she would walk and take in the sunshine. She put on her sun hat as she looked at herself in the mirror and laughed. *It may look silly but it would keep me from getting a sun burn,* she giggled. She gathered her things and started on her way.

She stopped at the little café and had a bowl of fruit and a cold espresso. She loved coming to the café. People were so nice to her there. Different then what she thought. She had heard from her coworkers. that Italians didn't like Americans and they had been treated poorly. She didn't think so. She would definitely come back and visit her new friends.

Her next stop was the museum. It was nice and cool inside, a nice break from the heat. She had forgotten how big it was. *I could spend all day in here.* The only word she could think of to describe the museum was magnificent. It was too bad cameras weren't allowed. She had found that out when Jenny and she tried to take pictures of them in here and the security came and erased the photos. That had made Jenny upset. Sarah laughed to herself remembering how Jenny's face looked. *Good times*, she said to herself.

"Excuse me?" Sarah asked the lady behind the customer service counter.

"Oh, my apologies. I didn't see you walk up. How may I help you?" the lady was very polite.

"I was looking for Frank. He had been doing some research for me. Do you know where I could find him?" Sarah asked. She studied the woman's face. She had to have been about her age, long brown hair and big brown eyes. Sarah envied the Italian women. They all seemed to have perfect skin, flawless even and the perfect shade of rose to their cheeks and lips.

"One moment, I'll get him for you," the

lady said as she started walking down the hall.

"Thank you," Sarah said quickly.

"Ahhhh Sarah. It's so good to see you," Frank said walking towards her as he held out his free hand to shake hers.

"You too," She loved how happy Italians were.

"I'm so glad you stopped by. I want to say first, that I haven't finished but why don't you come sit down with me so I can show you what I have so far. It's actually quite exciting and I'm so glad you came here for help. This project has come to be very interesting." And before Sarah could say anything he continued, "The items in the box you have are very old, dating back hundreds of years, at least to the 1600's if not older." Frank said with child-like excitement.

"Really? Wow." This information intrigued Sarah.

"Yes and the items, from what I could find out, are worth quite a bit of money. The dates put them in the era of the witch trials, which for someone like me, it makes me very excited. I haven't run across anything like this. You see, these pieces are even more impressive because of the witches they belonged too." He said with giddiness.

"Witches?" she asked with shock.

"Oh yes, you didn't know?" He asked puzzled.

"No. I was told very little. Just that these pieces had been in the family and to keep the research very low key."

"I can see why." He said with a non surprised voice. "Well, according to the legend that's written, there are two different lines here that I can tell."

"I don't follow."

"Witches are like any of us humans. They don't belong all together. They have their own covens, families if you will. When they find mates, they stick together until the end. They have rivals and they all have different abilities. There are good and bad ones and it says here that the bad ones tend to be more powerful." He said as he shifted through the papers showing Sarah chunks of paragraphs on each.

"But these are just stories, right?" Sarah asked in disbelief.

"Well to someone like you, yes I can see why you would think that, but for historians, like me, they aren't."

"I see," Sarah spoke with skepticism in her voice.

"Come, I have printed all the information that I have found so far for you. You don't mind if I continue looking up more information do you?" Frank asked as he started walking back to his office.

"No. Not at all," Sarah answered as she followed.

They entered his office and he motioned for her to sit at a small table in the corner as he cleared it off. His office was full of book shelves that were full of books. Books were stacked on top of more books and in every corner of the room. His desk was just as full. She wondered how he could find anything.

"Yes. I can find what I need. It's all in perfect order." He said as they both laughed. Sarah turned a little red with embarrassment from getting caught looking at the mess.

He sat down at the table with her and pulled out a folder from under the clutter. The folder was very full.

"Here is a copy of all the information I had found. I only told you some of the things. There is more in here," as he patted the folder and then slid it across the table.

"Thank you for all that you have done."

"Oh no thanks needed. I have loved doing this project. Here I wanted to show you this before you left." He said as he pulled out another folder labeled maps. "These are maps of old Italy and Sicily. I have highlighted the route the witches took to Sicily from Italy in yellow and the route back to Italy in blue."

"Why did they go to Sicily?"

"It all had to do with the annual meetings and witch hunts. It's all in the papers."

"Ok."

"Oh and the best thing, here is a picture of a castle on the route back to Italy that the witches took. There is a connection between them and the castle but I haven't gotten that far. Part of the reason I would like to continue. Anyway, I looked it up and the castle still stands, even after WWI but it's not listed on the historical list of places around Italy so it means that it's still privately owned. I took a drive past it and it is in impeccable condition. Here is the address and directions."

"Wait a minute!" Sarah said with excitement.

"What?"

"I think I have seen it. Does it have a huge wrought iron gate?"

"Yes."

"Yes! I have seen it. I rode a bike by there a few times. Stopped and looked at it, even took pictures of it myself. It had a creepy feel to it," Sarah got chills just thinking of it.

"Well with good reason."

"Why is that?" she asked.

"According to the legend, it belonged to the most evil of all witches back when the castle was built and it's said that the spirit of the witch still roams the castle."

"Really?"

"Yes. The so called connection with the

witches I was saying before, but at this point its just legend, I would need to find proof before I can say for sure and there's no record of who owns it now; which is strange."

Sarah wondered if Sophia knew this and that's why the secrecy but it didn't seem to her that Sophia knew anything by the way she acted. Besides, Sarah had to have the help from a historian to find this out.

"And that's why you want to keep working on it, to find proof?" Sarah asked.

"Yes."

"I don't see that as a problem, I leave at the end of the week, but you have my numbers," Sarah said.

"Good. I have a feeling that this is bigger then we know."

That made Sarah nervous. Not so much for her but for Sophia. She seemed skittish enough. But Sarah was intrigued by what more Frank could dig up.

"Ok well I will let you get back to work. Thank you again and keep me updated," Sarah said as she got up and put out her hand to shake Franks.

"I most definitely will," Frank said with a smile as he shook her hand and walked Sarah out into the hall.

"I can see myself out the rest of the way."

"Ok" Frank shrugged.

Sarah smile at Frank and walked down the hall towards the doors. She stopped at the service counter and thanked the lady for helping her and told her to have a nice day. She glanced down the hall and saw Frank still standing there watching her so she waved bye to him and walked out.

Sarah called Sophia but received her voice mail. She asked Sophia to meet her the next afternoon at the café that they had first met and a little after the noon hour. Sarah figured the next 24 hours would be plenty of time to look over the papers Frank had given her. Sarah thought it was pretty cool of Frank to do as much research as he had. She found it amusing how Frank wanted to continue to work on it even though he had basically did her job for her. She needed that help, there was no way she could have done it on her own. He had resources she didn't. By week's end she will be back home and although she loved being there, she was glad about going home. She hadn't been feeling good and needed to go to the doctors.

Sarah kept looking at her watch and looking around the outside of the café. No Sophia. It was almost 1. Maybe she didn't get the message. It was so bright out, so warm. She closed her eyes and looked up toward the sky letting the sun hit her face, warming it up. A dark shadow blocked the sun and it startled her. She heard a female laugh. Sarah opened her eyes to find Sophia sitting across from her.

"Sorry, I didn't mean to startle you," Sophia's soft voice said still smirking. She was wearing a huge sun hat. Biggest Sarah had ever seen. But even still, Sophia looked beautiful. Sarah wondered if she looked bad in anything. Sophia seemed like the type that could wear a paper bag and pull it off.

"No problem. Glad you made it." Sarah was relieved. Sarah waited until Sophia had settled in the chair before she started. The waiter came over to take her order but she passed on wanting anything. Sarah noticed that she didn't like the visits to be very long. She figured because of not wanting to be seen by her family.

"Well as I told you before, I had to get help from a historian, Frank, because of how far the items in the picture dated back to."

"I figured they were old but had no idea so old that you had to get a historian." Sophia was in awe of the work Sarah did. It went above and beyond what Sophia gave her credit for.

"Here is a copy of all the information both Frank and I found. I stuck the family tree in the front and then Frank's report in the back. There are maps of routes taken by your ancestors dating back to 1679, if you can believe that." Sarah still smiled at the fact that Frank was able to go back that far in history.

"Back that far?" Sophia was surprised by that.

"But that's not the most fascinating part," Sarah said as excitement was pouring out in her voice. "The neatest part I think, is that your ancestors were apart of the Roman Inquisition. Sophia…." Sarah paused not sure how Sophia will respond to what she was about to tell her.

"What is it? Go on please," Sophia was eager to know.

"Well, I think that the reason your family, your parents were so low key about your ancestors, your families past, was because your ancestors were dubbed witches."

Sophia gasped as she put a hand to cover her mouth. "No way!"

"Yes, it's all in this file." Sarah couldn't read Sophia, her reaction to the news. Sophia sat quiet while running her hand over the file.

"Witches, really?"

"Yes." Sarah said softly as she added that she would be there for the next couple of days before she leaves to go back home so if there was anything Sophia had questions on to feel free and stop by the apartment. Sophia thanked her again for all the help she had done and stood up, smiled at Sarah and started walking down the sidewalk; disappearing into the crowd. Sarah stared down the sidewalk until she could no longer see the big sun hat.

Something about the sun hat reminded Sarah that Sophia had given her an envelope when Jenny was there with her and it was still in the bag she had that day. *I'll look at it tonight when I get home*, she thought. She caught herself on the word home. For the first time she felt home sick. That amused her considering that when she left, she couldn't leave fast enough. Not because she didn't like being home but because of him, Luke, her neighbor. A feeling flashed over her. *No. how could I be, he is everything that I'm not,* her inner voice ranting on. But she failed to admit that she was becoming more drawn to him then she wanted. That she watched him as much as he watched her. She knew deep down that it might not have been entirely his fault for that one night. She was drunk, really drunk. *What if I had wanted him that night. What if the alcohol was like liquid courage for me?* Her mind wouldn't shut up. It was driving her crazy. Truth was, she wanted him. *The ultimate bad boy,* she thought.

She had no ideal just how much he watched her. In a twisted way she missed him. She felt like she thought of him more now then when she was at home. Maybe it was the Italian scenery, or the Hollywood romantic in her. *I need to stop watching all those chick flick romance movies,* she thought with a laugh. She thought she was getting it bad with Luke on the brain that she even thought she saw him one morning when she stepped out on the balcony of the apartment. Just standing there across the street looking up at her but by the time she could blink, he was gone. *I need more sleep, getting delirious,* she said to herself.

Enough of sitting here, I can only drink so much espresso on a hot day, she huffed as she stood up and put a tip on the table and headed back to the apartment. As she walked back she realized that she just may miss this place more then she let on. She felt carefree there. She only had a couple of nightmares while there. She pulled out her camera and started taking pictures on her route back to the apartment. When suddenly she couldn't shake the feeling that she was being followed, but when she looked around there was nothing that seemed out of the ordinary. She was feeling a little creeped out and she hated not being able to pick up the phone to call Jenny, unless of course she wanted an outrageous cell phone bill when she got back. Sarah wrinkled her nose at that thought. She had gotten use to writing nightly emails to Jenny and her boss, sometimes even being able to chat online with Jenny, but with the time difference, not often. Mr. Davis seemed to like getting her emails. He was a big history buff so this fascinated him. Sarah thought that maybe he was even a little jealous that she was there and not him. That made her smile.

Sarah made it back to the apartment and was happy to be there. She had spent most of the walk back looking over her shoulder and around the area she was in. She knew that she was being watched and she also knew that she wasn't just being paranoid. She locked the door and went about the apartment checking windows and rooms for anything out of the ordinary. When she was done, she sat down and admitted that maybe she had become a little paranoid and needed to get over that and soon before she became a crazy person. She knew one thing, when she gets back home she was going to confront Luke. She was done being creeped out by his actions. Sarah started not feeling well again and figured it being part of too much sun and the stress. She couldn't wait to get home. She thought about it and it seemed that she hadn't felt good in a couple of weeks. She had hoped it wasn't the flu.

Luke was standing across the street from Sarah's apartment when he saw a familiar vehicle pull up and park right outside Sarah's building. As Sophia got out of the car she took a quick look around. Luke ducked behind the column and watched Sophia go into the building.

"What is Sophia doing there? How does she know Sarah?" he spoke through clenched teeth. He didn't recall seeing them run into each other around town. He needed to know what was going on. He took the stairs to the third floor like he had done a few times before and walked up to Sarah's door. He could hear muffled voices coming from inside. It upset him that he couldn't hear. He was mad that he couldn't use his abilities because of his sister being in there, not knowing what he was. He heard the elevator ding, someone was coming out so he started walking in the opposite direction.

Not more then a few minutes after Luke got back into the spot, he had been standing in, before Sophia appear from the building. *That was close,* he sighed. She didn't visit for long, which seemed odd to Luke. He waited until he could no longer see Sophia's car before emerging from behind the column. He went back into the building and back up to her apartment. To his surprise the door was cracked open. He wondered if Sophia just didn't shut it all the way. He slowly walked up closer when he could hear Sarah talking to someone. One sided conversation, *she was on the phone,* his inner voice concluded.

"No she just left," he heard her say. "She just wanted to know where page 12-20 was. No, No, I'll be gone by then. She said that she would just stop by in a couple of days to get it from you. Yes, yes she is," Sarah finished laughing. Luke wondered what that meant. *Who was she talking too?* He heard her walking around and then water turning on, sounded like the bathtub. He carefully pushed open the door and entered the apartment. Lucky for him he could use his abilities and could move about without making a sound. He could see she had a glass of what smelled like ice tea. He pulled out a little metal container no bigger then the size of a dime and emptied the contents into the glass and watched as it dissolved. *Perfect for tonight, if she drinks it that is,* he thought. He heard the bathroom door open. He quickly ducked out on to the balcony and watched her come into view. She was only wrapped in a towel. His body was instantly begging for her. *She looked...she was... stop it. Focus Luke*, he told himself. He watched her grab her drink from the counter and back into the bathroom shutting the door behind her. *Well that was easy*, he thought. He looked around and noticed from past visits that the paperwork was no longer on the table. *Shoot should have looked at it when I had the chance before,* he said to himself. He went into the bedroom and saw her suitcases out and one was packed. This visit was unsuccessful in finding out what was going on. He had a few hours before the powder took effect and decided to come back then.

Sarah relaxed into a nice hot bubble bath, closed her eyes for no more then five minutes when her cell rang. She quickly dried her hands off and looked at the screen, it was Jenny.

"Hello!" Sarah said happy that Jenny called.

"Hey chicka, oh wait wrong country, it's Bella right now," Jenny answered with a giggle.

"Didn't expect to hear from you today," Sarah was surprised by the call.

"I know, but with you leaving in a few days I wanted you to know that I'm going out of town for a night or two with Robert and wanted to touch base with you before I left," Jenny explained.

"Oh, where are you two love birds going?"

"I don't know. Robert is surprising me, but don't worry I will be back in time to pick you up."

"I'm not worried Jen, hope you two have fun."

"I will," Jenny sounded very happy.

"Oh wow."

"What's wrong?" Jenny asked.

"I just got really tired, or maybe got to hot sitting in this tub. I don't know," Sarah said feeling loopy.

"Why don't you go lie down for a while, get some rest." Jenny said with the motherly voice Sarah was so use to hearing.

"I will. I'm going to get out now," Sarah said knowing that sleep would probably be best. They said their goodbyes and hung up.

Oh man, I must have drifted off to sleep, Sarah thought as she pulled herself up into a sitting position. She unplugged the drain and slowly got out, wrapped herself in a towel and opened the door to the bathroom. It was getting dark in the apartment but Sarah didn't care, she was going to bed. She felt groggy and if she didn't know any better she would think she had been drugged. She chalked it up to no sleep and put the glass away in the kitchen and started stumbling down the hall towards to the bedroom. Something caught her attention behind her and she turned around real quick but there was nothing. Disgusted with herself and her paranoia, she went into the bedroom, shut the door and crawled into bed. Her eyes were so heavy. *Must be more tired then I thought,* her inner voice said. Sarah's eyes closed.

Sarah's eyes opened, it was dark. Her heart started pounding. She couldn't move. *Oh no*, she thought. She instantly looked at the foot of her bed and there it was, the dark shadow. She could feel tears filling her eyes. Something moved on the side of her, panic set in. *Two dark shadows? What is going on?* The dark shadow on the side of her moved closer to her, but it didn't give off the creepy feel that the one at the foot of the bed did and the closer it got, the more the creepy one felt less of a threat. The shadow next to her, bent down towards her face. It was Luke. *She had to be dreaming,* she thought. Fear was being replaced with a different kind of feeling. Her body felt hot, wanting Luke to touch it.

"As the creeeper twines the tree, so your arms will twine round me in deepest love. As the eagle rides the wind, so do I control your mind to deepest love. As the sun rules every part, so do I possess your heart in deepest love," Luke whispered in Italian into Sarah's ear a spell he had found in a book from Damien's library long ago. She didn't know exactly what he said nor did she care. It made her body heat up, she wanted him. She turned her face toward his as he swept his lips over her cheek and on to her lips.

"Wait!" Sarah said as she pulled her lips away from Luke's. He just kept his eyes locked on to hers. She looked at the foot of her bed, the dark shadow was gone. Luke looked in the same direction as Sarah and then back at her, never saying a word.

"There was a dark shadow over there," Sarah pointed.

Luke didn't say anything; he figured it was him that she was talking about. He smiled. He uncovered her slowly as he ran a hand over her freshly tanned body. His touch was slow, soft and meticulous. He knew what he was doing. She felt her body heat up more. She loved these kinds of dreams. She had come to want Luke. Sarah closed her eyes and gave in fully to him, as he made love to her, so completely, until she felt like a hundred bombs going off inside her as she yelled out his name.

How does she know my name, he wondered, but stayed quiet otherwise that would ruin it, ruin everything. He laid there with her, his arms wrapped around her body. He didn't want to leave but he knew he had too before it wore off. He slowly slid his arms out from under her and got out of the bed. He got dressed and then went back to Sarah's side. He gently kissed her forehead and watched her for a moment longer. She looked so beautiful, so peaceful. He knew he was falling in love with her. He didn't know how long he could fool Damien.

Chapter 11

Sarah was relieved when the airplane touched down. It meant she was finally home. It had been a month in Italy, and although it had been a chance of a lifetime and met some wonderful people, she would definitely keep in touch with and go back to visit. She missed the U.S. She picked up her luggage and headed to the parking garage. Jenny was supposed to meet her there.

As she stood there waiting in roughly the same spot that Jenny had dropped her off, she couldn't help but have an uneasy feeling standing in the cold, dimly lit garage. She glanced around, it was full of cars and in the distance she could see and hear people walking away from their cars and going into the airport, and she wondered where they were going. After they entered it got real creepy. She could hear faint screeching of tires on another level of the garage. She looked around again, she couldn't shake the feeling that she was being watched.

He was two car rows away from her. He had flown in on the flight before her. He wanted to be there to watch her. She wasn't going to get out of his sight again. He was in her apartment in Italy when she had a conversation with her friend on the phone making arrangements for getting picked up. He was glad that he decided to go that evening. Now that they were back in the states he could have her all to himself. No worrying about running into his family or Damien. He wondered how much she knew when she was helping his sister. He wondered why his sister was looking up their families past. He had seen the family tree Sarah had hanging in the bedroom. He was half tempted to rip it down but had to be careful not to disturb anything. He didn't want to alert her. He liked the element of surprise and he liked that he had made her jumpy, scared. She should be. She should be afraid of him. He wanted her to be afraid of him; it would be easier for him to hate her that way. He hated that he was developing feelings for her. He should just go kill her and be done with it. His thoughts were all over the place and his hands were tightening around the steering wheel.

Just as he built up the anger needed and put his car into gear, Sarah's friend showed up to pick her up. She was driving Sarah's car. *That figures,* he thought as he watched them pull out. He followed them. They went to Jenny's house. Sarah went in and stayed a while. After she left she made stops at her job, the grocery store, the post office and then home. He waited down the road until he saw her pull into her garage and then quickly pulled into his before he was seen. Little did he know the Wilson's saw. They saw everything that happened on their road, at least that's what they thought. They had failed to see all the times Luke had gone next door.

Sarah was so glad to be home. She missed her house. She put her bags upstairs and all her mail on the counter and unpacked her groceries. She was exhausted and all she wanted to do was sleep, after a bath of course. That was an all day travel and she felt dirty. She made sure everything was locked up tight and went upstairs, decided on a shower and then crawled into bed and passed right out.

Sarah woke up the next day thankful that she didn't have a nightmare. It still looked a little dark in the room, having been so use to the bright sun in Italy. She got out of bed and peaked out her window, cloudy. *I miss the sun already*, she huffed. She looked across at Luke's house; the blinds were drawn in all the windows on that side of the house. She wondered what he was doing, wondered if he wondered where she had been. Sarah let out a little sigh, turned and walked out of her room.

That was close, he thought as he tried to shake off the exhaustion that happens after transposing oneself. He had every intention on scaring her but got so caught up just watching her that she woke up before he realized that the morning had come. He knew one thing after that night, he couldn't kill her, and unfortunately he wasn't the only one that knew that. He was so wrapped up watching her that he had failed to see that he was being watched as well. Damien was there too, watching Luke watch Sarah. Damien could no longer trust Luke to take care of what needed to be done. He would take care of it himself.

Even though Sarah missed the sun and the warmth, she was glad to be home. She stood in the shower longer then normal. She wasn't nearly as creeped out about being home as she was before she left for Italy. Sarah started feeling sick. She quickly got out of the shower, making it to the toilet just in time to throw up. She waited in the bathroom until her stomach subsided.

She called the doctors and was able to get in that afternoon. She really didn't want to go out but needed to get this flu bug taken care of. She went downstairs and made coffee and some toast and it seemed to calm her stomach down a bit. She went through the big stack of mail, nothing of importance.

Before Sarah left she went across the street to the Wilson's but no one answered. *That's odd*, Sarah thought, *they are always home this time of day, guess I'll just come back later.* She walked down the Wilson's driveway and stopped at the sidewalk staring at Luke's house. *Why am I falling for someone so dark? How is that possible?* She wondered. Not realizing it she walked over to Luke's house. She hesitated at the front door to listen for any sounds or movements from inside. There was nothing; only silence. With a shaky hand, she knocked. Her heart was racing and the sick feeling was coming back. *You can do this*, she said to herself.

She didn't hear anything, no sounds from a television, a radio, no footsteps, no lights, just dark and silence. *Oh well*, she thought with relief. She turned to walk away when she heard the door open. She turned around. Nobody was there but the door was cracked open. Against her better judgment she walked back up to it.

"Hello?" She called out but nothing back. She wondered if she should go in or not but curiosity got the better of her. She pushed the door open. It was dark inside with the curtains shut and it was eerily quiet. She felt goose bumps forming on her arms. She left the door open for light and a quick exit if needed. Sarah entered the living room and called out hello once more but again just silence, it didn't appear that he was home.

Part of her told her to leave and the other said to stay and look around. The daring, nosy side won. Feeling her heart speed up, *ok maybe the stupid part of me,* she thought. She knew the layout already so she went to the garage just to make sure Luke's car was gone. It was. Everything in the garage was immaculate. *I could eat off the cement ground.* There was a cover on what appeared to be a motorcycle. She walked over and uncovered half the bike and ran her hand ever so softly and slowly across it. It was beautiful and sleek, black of course. She wondered if he owned anything with color. Sarah's thought made her laugh. The truth was is that half of her wardrobe was either black or dark brown. She wondered what it would be like sitting on the back of it with her arms wrapped around his waist tight. She quickly covered it back up and went back into the house. She opened the back door and looked around. Nothing. She left that door open too, for another escape route. She went back through the living room and headed upstairs. She went into the bedroom she hadn't been in before and unfortunate for her, it was on the back side of the house. She didn't hear the front door close.

Sarah liked this room. It wasn't dark like the rest of the house. It was inviting. She walked over to the bed, which reminded her of the bed in Italy. It was draped in ivory satin and white goose down and had a lot of pillows. She sat down on the bed, leaned over and opened the night stand table. Empty. She figured the other one was the same and didn't bother checking. The bed was so soft; she laid back on it just to see how comfortable it was. She wondered who he had as guests. She got up and walked over to the dresser. Every drawer was empty and same with the closet. Definitely a guest room but even her guest room had stuff in it like a robe and some knick knacks for the guests to feel at home.

She went to the next door down the hall, the third bedroom but it appeared that he made it into an office. A computer desk took up one wall and there were a lot of monitors on it. They were all off. *Wonder what those are for?* She thought. Little did she know they were to watch her and the neighbors. Luke had to know when it was the right time to go over. She tried to open the desk drawers but they were locked, same with the cabinet next to the desk. That made her more curious as to what was in them to keep them locked when he was the only one that lived there. She moved on to the next door, she already knew what it was, the bathroom and skipped it. She stood outside the last door, the only room she knew. She had a flash back of the last time she was in that room as she put her hand on the door knob. It gave her the chills to think about it. She heard a creak behind her coming from the stairs and she jumped, her heart started pounding hard in fear. She froze; her eyes glanced over to the staircase anticipating someone to show up any second. But there was nothing. She slowly walked over and with just her head peaked around the corner. No one was there. She couldn't see the light hitting the stairs from the opened front door. She stayed perfectly still, even holding her breath, she couldn't hear anything. She exhaled, *maybe it was a gust of wind that closed the door*, she breathed as she slowly started going back down the stairs, inching along the wall; still no sounds from downstairs. Sarah was on the last landing of the stairs when she saw a shadow move along the wall right pass the front door which was indeed shut. Her heart skipped a beat and started pounding harder but she still didn't hear anything, maybe it was a car passing by and the sunlight, what little was out, caught the reflection of the metal and that's what she saw, she thought to herself, knowing that's not what it was because there had been no sound of a vehicle. As she was telling herself to get a grip, she slowly went down the rest of the way and stopped to listen again, still nothing. She slowly stuck her head around the corner and she could see a shadow going into the kitchen and a sick panic feeling rushed through her, and for the first time in over a month, she felt scared.

Stepping as softly as she could she went to the front door and turned the knob very slowly as to not make any noise while looking back over her shoulder. She noticed that the back door that was just open a minute ago was now shut. That sent fear rippling through her body and she started feeling sick again. She couldn't get the door open fast enough and get through the door. She shut the door quickly behind her and started walking down the walkway when she froze. There pulling into the drive was the black sleek car she had seen only a couple of times before.

Oh god what do I say, get composure of yourself, quick, calm, stay calm, she couldn't shut her inner voice up.

Sarah stood there watching as the car came to a screeching stop. She didn't move; she was terrified. Her heart felt like it was going to explode and she didn't know if it was because of the fact that she was just in his house and she knew she wasn't alone, or the fact that she barely got out of there when he arrived home, or because he was in his car only a few feet from her and he hadn't gotten out yet, or the combination of all. She didn't know and at this point none of it mattered because her heart was going to explode. *What is he doing in there? Why hasn't he gotten out? Why won't my feet move? I must look stupid just standing here. Shut up, just shut up, auugghh,* Sarah thought as she argued with her inner voice.

What is she doing? Why is she here? If I hadn't have come home so quickly maybe I would have missed her. What am I going to say to her. Have to be cold, make her leave. I can't, I don't want her to go. Look how beautiful she is, the way the black sundress looks on her. Hmmm, nice color. Better get this over with, his mind was all over the place. He hated feeling out of control. He needed to keep his distance. If Damien ever knew he was falling for her, he would end her life. Luke shook his head in confusion of it all. It was beginning to be too much. His cell phone rang. What timing he thought as he looked at the number. It was his sister Sophia. He hit ignore so the call would go to voicemail. She called right back and again he hit ignore and then turned it off. He felt his heart beat pick up when he opened the car door.

The door to his car started opening and Sarah felt like she was going to pass out. She watched as his feet hit the pavement. *Nice shoes had to be expensive.* She watched as he slowly got out of his car and shut the door and hit the alarm on the remote control. He was absolutely gorgeous; from his dark shiny hair to his perfect olive skin tone. He was tall and through his body hugging clothes, she could see that he was in perfect shape. Just like her dreams of him. She felt weak. *What am I doing here? Why did I come over here? Should have left earlier, wouldn't be in this position now,* she thought as she let out a sign. He stopped in front of her. She could feel her heart skip a beat. *Think I'm going to faint, please don't come any closer*, her inner voice said. Then he spoke.

"What do you want?" he scowled. That surprised Sarah a little bit. He's nothing like she had dreamt he would be. She was a little disappointed in that.

"Uh, I…Umm…I just…" She couldn't talk. *What is wrong with me? I sound stupid. Get it together*, she thought. She took a deep breath and tried to start again but he beat her to it.

"WHAT?" he said trying to sound as mean as he could and by the look on Sarah's face, it seem to be working. It made Sarah a little upset that he was being so rude.

"I just came over to introduce myself but I see that was a mistake so NEVERMIND," she said as she gave him her look of death. He had to hold a straight face but it was hard. He thought she was so cute trying sound like it didn't bother her. She started to walk away from him, back towards her house. He watched her as she walked past him and crossed over to her yard.

"Wait," he shouted at her. She froze and waited for him to say more. He didn't. He waited for her to turn around and after a moment she did. They stood there just staring at each other. It was like nothing else was around them. They both knew they had feelings for the other but neither would say so.

"Would you come inside?" He asked with a much softer voice.

"Why should I? You were pretty rude just now," she responded with a bit of a snooty tone to hers.

That started to upset him. *Why is she being so difficult?* He thought, "Then don't" he started to snarl again.

Sarah didn't know what to do. She was afraid to go back into his house. But he was home and maybe whatever it was that was in there is now gone. She may never have an opportunity again to be invited in. *Go stupid! What are you waiting for*, she could hear Jenny's voice yelling at her. *Great not only do I have to fight my own mind but I have Jenny's in there as well?* With a deep breath, she walked back over. He turned and walked towards the door to his house. *I sure hope I locked it behind me*, she thought as they reached the door. She held her breath as he went to unlock the door. She slowly took a breath again, *good it was*.

He held the door open and he motioned for her to enter. She got chills when she walked passed him, glancing at him. He had the most beautiful brown eyes she had ever seen. She quickly looked away. He shut the door behind her and walked over to the window and opened the curtains letting the light shine throughout the room. Even though the colors were on the darker side, it felt strangely comfortable to her and yet she couldn't calm her heart rate down. She felt confused about everything. He again motioned for her to do something, this time to sit on the couch. She complied. She sat down feeling a little awkward as to how to sit. She wanted to sit on the edge of the cushion in case she had to get up fast but didn't want to give off the wrong impression so she decided to sit all the way back trying to look like she was ok about being there. That made him chuckle inside, he knew she was uncomfortable, it showed. So, he sat down next to her on the couch.

A weird tension filled the air between the two of them. Not because they didn't want to be next to each other, it was more of this unexplained chemistry they could feel towards each other.

"I'm Luke," he said as he held out his hand to Sarah.

"I'm Sarah," she said as she put her hand into his to shake it. There was this feeling she had never felt before. It shot through her entire body. They sat there looking straight into each other's eyes still holding each others hand.

"Hi," he whispered with a crack of a smile on his face. *He was so beautiful*, she thought as her body started heating up.

"Hi," she whispered back and then she couldn't help herself, "I've seen you watching me, why?"

"Hmm," he grunted, let go of her hand and got up. She got up quickly as a reflex to his action, not sure if she should be going for the door or not. Seeing her reaction, he smiled, *still have that affect on her I see,* he thought. His smile turned to a frown, *I don't want that, I want her so bad it hurts deep down to the core of my body, it hurts.* She started heading to the door but he stopped her. It startled her.

"Don't go," he whispered in her ear. She was at the door facing it and he was standing right behind her with his arms on each side of her resting on the door. She didn't know if she should be afraid of him or not. She was having a hard time reading his actions. She turned around slowly looking directly into his eyes. She felt sick. His eyes looked sad, tormented even.

"Why do you want me to stay? You scowl at me when you talk to me. Do you not want to know me?" her inner voice telling her not to keep asking questions but she couldn't stop. "Why are you always watching me?"

He was so close to her. She could feel parts of his body touching her. He looked irritated by all the questions. She thought maybe he regretted asking her in when he did something that shocked her so much it took her breath away. He wrapped her face into his hands and drew her in. He laid the most passionate kiss on her she had ever experienced, way more then she imagined in her dream. The feeling of sickness got stronger... *Are you kidding me,* she thought.

He leaned against her body, *No not against my stomach, not going to get sick, not going to get sick, no,* she kept telling herself. He ran a hand down her side and around to the small of her back and pulled her into him tight. She wanted to melt in his arms. She knew nothing about him and there were things that needed answering. There was a dark feeling about him, like she knew she should be afraid of him but didn't know why and yet wanted him, this stranger next door. The sickness was becoming too great. She broke his hold.

"I'm sorry," she turned away from him and started to open the door.

"Don't go," Luke whispered.

"I have too," She whispered back as she held a hand to her mouth. She opened the door and without looking back, she left Luke standing there with a confused look on his face.

Sarah went back into her house and locked the door behind her. She noticed the time; it was time for her to go. The sick feeling grew; she made it to the bathroom just in time. She gathered her things and left for the doctors.

Chapter 12

It seemed like she waited in the little examination room for a long time after having every test ran on her. She felt like a guinea pig. She heard a little knock at the door letting her know it was the doctor coming in.

"Well Sarah let's see what we have here," the doctor said as he opened up her file as he continued on, "we wont know the blood work for a couple of days but I think I know what's going on without those results."

"The flu?" she asked.

"No, here is a prescription for prenatal vitamins" he said handing her a piece of paper.

"What?" Sarah didn't think she heard him right.

"You're pregnant."

She was in shock. The doctor kept talking but Sarah tuned him out while she processed what he first said. *Pregnant? That can't be.*

"Sarah?" The doctor asked trying to get her attention. "Sarah?"

"Hmm," she half heartily answered.

"From what you have told my nurse about your cycle my guess is that your about 6 weeks along. I would like you to come back in a month and get a sonogram to check things out and get a better idea of a due date."

"Ok," was all Sarah could say. The doctor left and in a blur Sarah got dressed and left herself. In a daze she picked up her prenatal pills and chocolate ice cream and before she knew it, she was sitting in her car that was already parked in her garage. *Oh my.* She got out of her car and went inside. She sat on her couch staring at the bottle of pills on the coffee table. Her cell phone started ringing. The number didn't look familiar so she let it go to voice mail. *Jenny, got to call Jenny.* She picked up the cell and dialed Jenny.

"Hey Sarah," Jenny answered happy to have her friend back, but there was only silence. "Sarah?"

"Jen, I need you," Sarah whispered.

"Sarah what's wrong?"

"Come please."

"I'm on my way," Jenny hung up the phone and swiped her keys off the counter and sped towards Sarah's house. It took half the time it normally would have and she was thankful that no police officers were on the route she took. She was worried about Sarah and there was only two other times she had heard that tone in Sarah's voice. She remembered them like it was yesterday.

The first time was when they were little kids and Sarah had come to stay the night and she was very quiet and sad. When it was time to go to bed Sarah was laying there quietly crying and when she asked why; Sarah told her that her parents were fighting so much that she had to stay the night at her uncle's house and his friend had touched her. Jenny hugged Sarah all night, she cried along with her. Sarah had made Jenny promise never to tell anyone, and she never did.

The second time was a call in the middle of the night, Sarah was crying to the point of incomprehension. When Jenny finally calmed Sarah down enough to find out what was wrong it even through her for a loop. Her parents had gotten in a horrific car accident, both died. There were other calls but to the extent to hear that certain tone in Sarah's voice meant something bad had happened. She was so thankful for no police.

Sarah had gotten up to unlock the front door knowing her friend and how long it would take for Jenny to get there after that call; her distress call. She wouldn't know what to do without Jenny in her life. She heard the front door open then shut. She didn't need to look up to know her friend had arrived. Jenny took a seat next to her on the couch.

"Sarah? What's wrong?" Jenny asked pushing Sarah's hair aside revealing a tear stained face.

Sarah leaned forward toward the table and picked up the bottle and placed it in Jenny's hands and started crying again. Jenny looked down at the bottle and her mouth dropped as Sarah whispered, "I'm pregnant."

"Oh Sarah," Jenny said as she wrapped her arm around Sarah's shoulders and pulled her close and let her friend cry. "How far along are you?"

"About 6 weeks."

Jenny didn't have to ask anymore. She did the math and realized why she was crying. It was Mr. Creepy's baby. She hugged Sarah a little tighter. They sat there in silence for a long time.

"Does he know?"

"No."

"Want some tea? I want some tea," Jenny said getting up. She was freaking out inside and didn't want Sarah to see so she went into the kitchen and started making tea before Sarah could respond. Sarah knew her friend was freaking out but staying strong for her sake. She also knew that if she hurt then Jenny hurt too. She loved her friend.

Sarah sat in shock staring at the bottle of pills, *I'm pregnant? What am I going to do? Do I tell Jenny about my encounter with Luke before I had gone to the doctors?* She had so many questions and her inner voice wasn't helping.

She could hear Jenny making tea and knew she had to tell her.

"Jenny?"

"Be right there, the tea is almost done."

"Ok, but there's something else I need to tell you."

"You already told me you're pregnant, what else is there?" Jenny said with worry.

Sarah didn't answer Jenny's comment. She turned her attention to the front door. She could hear someone walking up to the porch. She waited for the knock thinking it was probably Luke coming over to finish what they started earlier or confront her on her quick exit.

The door was kicked open, startling Sarah as she jumped up to a standing position letting out a scream. Hearing Sarah, Jenny dropped the cups of tea and as they went crashing down on the tiled floor Jenny came flying around the corner to a dead stop. Her mouth dropped. Sarah ran over to Jenny and stood in front of her with her arms straight out from her sides as if to protect Jenny.

There stood two old men. The one in front was much older and shorter then the one behind him. They were both dressed in dark medieval clothing like someone who just stepped off the set from a Hollywood movie about warlocks; the only difference is the two old men were wearing the actual clothing from that era. The shorter one held a cane that had a silver claw hand wrapped over the top and he had gray hair.

The other had salt and pepper hair. Something caught Sarah's eyes. It was a ring the shorter one wore. She had seen that ring before, just hours before. Luke had one just like it. Sarah was terrified. They looked like very bad men. She knew Jenny well enough to know she had to be just as scared.

"Who the hell are you?" Sarah yelled at the two old creepy looking men standing in her living room. The taller of the two men stood behind the shorter one. The shorter one much older started chanting something in Italian, neither answering. Both the women had fear ripping through them. Sarah stood in front of Jenny as if to protect her.

"Get out of my house!" Sarah demanded. The men only moved closer forcing the women to move back, which was ok because they were trying to move back towards the back door.

"You heard her, GET OUT!" Jenny yelled as she got in front of Sarah. "GET OUT!" Jenny yelled again taking a step toward the men. Sarah reached out to grab her arm but Jenny was faster and moved out of reach. Within a blink of an eye the taller man had Jenny held back by the couch. Jenny was yelling at him; a lot of obscenities. The older man was chanting louder and louder and he was raising his arms. Sarah was terrified.

"What the hell is going on?" Sarah yelled at the old creepy man. She wanted to run but she wasn't going to leave Jenny.

"Say good bye to your friend," the taller man said in Jenny's ear.

"Sarah run!" Jenny yelled at her friend. She started to cry.

"I'm not leaving without you."

"The baby! Please go," Jenny pleaded with her. That caught the shorter man's attention and he started chanting louder with a meaner tone.

"NOT without you!" Sarah yelled back. Just then the back door flung open. Sarah turned sideways to see who was coming in. She took a deep breath in, *LUKE!*

"Damien don't you dare hurt her!" Luke scowled at the short old creepy man. Sarah's relief turned to confusion.

"You know him?" Sarah yelled at Luke pushing him as he tried to step in front of her to block Damien's spell of death that he was casting on her. The push knocked him a foot away from her. Luke started to stumble but quickly recovered. Sarah caught movement from the back door and turned to look as Frank and Sophia came running in.

"What the hell is going on," Sarah yelled looking around at everyone ending with the old man chanting something in Italian. Frank reached Sarah and grabbed her arms from behind and started pulling her back. She was resisting, turning her head towards Frank.

"Let me go!" she yelled at him, yanking free.

"No. Come on, NOW!" Frank yelled

back at Sarah.

Sarah didn't see what Jenny, Sophia and Luke saw; the horror that was in their eyes. The women started screaming as Luke jumped in front of Sarah. Sarah turned her head back towards Luke but what caught her eye had her looking over his shoulder at the old man, who had just released a dagger from his hand and for a split second all the chaos stopped, it was silent, Sarah felt herself screaming, but she didn't hear a sound.

The dagger came across the room so fast that Luke couldn't react. Luke looked down seeing the handle of the dagger as it sank into his chest. He looked back up at Damien, who looked satisfied enough with what he had done. Luke wrapped his hands around the handle and fell to his knees. Jenny elbowed the taller man in the stomach as hard as she could and felt him buckle over in pain. She quickly ran over to where Sarah was. Sarah and Sophia were screaming and crying, Frank pulled out his cell phone and called 911, and the old men took the distraction and chaos as their way out and disappeared.

Sarah started to go to her knees when Luke started to fall back. She caught him and held him in her lap with her arms wrapped around him.

"Luke," Sarah whispered sobbing. Sophia was sobbing uncontrollably next to Sarah holding Luke's arm.

"Sarah Beautiful Sarah," Luke tried choking out the words.

"Don't talk, save your energy," Frank demanded.

"Sarah listen," Luke said paying no mind to Frank. Sarah bent her head down closer to Luke.

"Those nights you thought you were having nightmares. You weren't dreaming. I was there. I was really making love to you and it was me, the dark shadow, which taunted you at the foot of your bed" Luke said trying to fight the pain that was ripping through his body. *She deserved to know the truth even if at the cost of her hating me,* he thought.

"What?" Sarah whispered. She was so confused, "you're behind those horrible nightmares? You're the one who hurt me?"

"No, that was Damien, the one standing over there. The one who did this to me," Luke trying to point to Damien but he was fading fast.

"They're gone!" Jenny yelled. Sarah didn't care.

"I just watched you. I mean at first I tried to scare you, wanted to hurt you but I couldn't. He found out and tried to hurt you, I couldn't do it…" Luke said fading, his eyes starting to close.

"Do what?" Sarah said as she shook Luke to make him stay awake.

"Kill you," he said softly as his eyes were closing more. Sarah gasped.

"Kill her?" Sophia asked, "What is going

on Luke?" Sophia was just as confused as Sarah.

"Why? Luke? Why?" Sarah shook him. *This was all too much.* Sarah's head was spinning.

"The curse."

"What? What are you talking about?" Sarah shook Luke harder, but Luke was losing consciousness.

"Luke wake up!" Sarah yelled.

"Luke? No! Luke you stay with us," Sophia sobbed shaking her brother's arm. Jenny and Frank stood over them in disbelief. The sounds of sirens were getting louder.

"Don't you die on me!" Sarah spit out in between crying fits.

The police came in with their guns out.

"The intruders left. We don't know where they went. There's two of them, old men, one of them stabbed him and then disappeared," Jenny said very quickly. She was afraid the police officers were going to think they were the bad guys.

"Stay there," one of the officers barked as he and his partner went upstairs to check. They could hear them clearing each room and in just a few moments were back downstairs. Once they cleared the house they went outside to let the paramedics know it was ok to enter.

"Luke, wake up, wake up, please. WAKE

UP!" Sarah was crying hysterically while shaking Luke. Her head bent down next to his; touching cheek to cheek. Her tears ran down her face and on to his.

"Ma'am, I'm sorry but you need to move so we can help him," one of the medics said.

"Help him please," Sarah begged whispering but not moving.

"You need to move," the other medic said sternly.

Sarah couldn't bare to let go, even though she knew she had too. She was worried that it would be the last time she would see him. She felt so confused and although she just found out he wanted to kill her, but didn't, she still wanted him. She had fallen for him. She didn't know if she even wanted the baby a few hours ago but now she knew. She wanted this baby more then anything this world could give her. It tied Luke to her, even if he was dying.

Jenny pulled Sarah back so the medics could do their job and hopefully, for Sarah's sake, save Luke, even though Jenny was now more then ever not very fond of Luke. Sophia was crying in Frank's arms and Frank couldn't believe what was happening. He hadn't told Sophia and Luke everything. He had just begun to tell them that when he was doing his own family ancestry found out he was related to the Moretti family; that their ancestors were cousins when they heard screaming coming from Sarah's house and Luke went running with him and Sophia in tow and everything else happened so fast. He thought the mystical family tale was just a tale, he never thought it was real and now wouldn't be the time to tell the others what he knew.

Sarah was sobbing uncontrollably in Jenny's arms watching the paramedics trying to revive Luke. But they didn't seem to be doing much she thought, which only made her cry harder.

"Please don't let him die," she pleaded with the medics but they didn't seem to hear her.

The medics quickly loaded Luke on to a stretcher and flew out the door and down the driveway to the ambulance. Sarah and Jenny were the first ones out of the house followed by Frank and Sophia. The police stopped the four of them at the start of the walkway wanting to know what happened and who the two were that stabbed Luke. Sarah was having none of it and only cared to keep Luke in her sight.

"Sarah go. I'll take this," Frank said nudging Sarah on. She didn't wait to find out if the police were ok with that. She grabbed Sophia's hand and led her down to the ambulance. They made it to the back door of the ambulance as one of the medics shut the door and headed to the drivers side. Sarah tried talking to him but he only waved her off. She joined Sophia in looking into the back window. She gasped at the sight. She saw the other medic putting an IV into him and using a bag to help him breath.

"GO, GO, GO!!" they heard the medic yell to the driver. The lights and sirens turned on and the ambulance sped off down the street.

Sarah and Sophia held each other, both crying watching the ambulance leave.

"Sarah they need you to give a statement on what happened," Jenny said trying to comfort her friend.

"I need to go," Sarah said sobbing, pulling against Jenny, following Sophia to the car parked against the curb. The police followed all of them to the car.

"Ma'am! We need to talk to you. We need a statement," one of them said. Sarah ignored everyone and got in the car.

"Can't you do it later?" Frank asked.

"Tell you what, you guys can follow us to the hospital and we can do it there," the officer said seeing how distraught Sarah was.

The other three piled into the car and waited for the police car to go in front. Sarah had been crying so hard that the lights from the police car were nothing but a blur. *Why was this happening to me? What was this all about? I'm so confused. I don't understand,* her inner voice couldn't be silenced, *Why was Frank and Sophia here? Why were they with Luke? LUKE! God what's happening to him?* Her mind wouldn't shut off. Like the lights, the ride to the hospital was a blur as well. She could hear the others talking but she couldn't focus on their conversation; the voice in her head was louder trying to make sense of everything that just took place. Her eyes were starting to swell from all the crying and her heart was racing. *I just saw Luke a few hours ago, I'm pregnant with his baby, and now he's dying or worse, dead*, Sarah started into another crying fit.

They arrived at the hospital and Sarah jumped out before Sophia could put the car in park. She raced into the emergency room entrance and up to the desk.

"Can I help you?" the lady sitting at the desk asked.

"I'm here for Luke. I mean he was brought in" Sarah was stumbling on her words.

"What's his last name?" the lady asked.

"Uhhh, Luke, Ah..." Sarah didn't know, she didn't know what to say when it was said for her.

"Luciano Moretti," Sophia said. Sarah turned around and gave Sophia a look of confusion, "Luke is my brother." Sarah was floored. *Too much, way too much is happening at once,* Sarah thought.

"Brother?" Sarah whispered in shock.

"Are you family?" the lady asked Sarah and without thinking Sarah said no.

"Only family can have access to patients in this ER. You, come with me." The lady said to Sophia and she led her behind a set of double doors and disappeared. Sarah stood there trying to process all of it when she felt someone tug on her arm, she jumped.

"Ma'am I'm sorry but we need to talk to

you. We can do it here or we can take you to the station. Your decision," the officer said in a stern voice. Sarah's heart was racing more then it had ever done before, she couldn't catch her breath, and she was feeling sick to her stomach. She turned to talk to the officers when everything went dark.

Chapter 13

"Sarah! Sarah!" Luke yelled out. He was running over to Sarah's house. He kicked the back door in and saw Damien casting a spell on Sarah and Salvator holding her friend over by the couch. *NO!,* he heard himself yell out. He watched as Damien pulled out a dagger from his coat and threw it towards Sarah. Luke ran in front of Sarah just in time as the dagger sank into his chest. *OH GOD!* He thought as he could feel pain rip through his body dropping him to his knees. Everything went black. He couldn't see anything but he could hear people crying, people talking fast, loud noises he couldn't make out. Then suddenly everything went dark.

"Sarah! Sarah!" He yelled out. He was running over to Sarah's house. He slowed. He remembers doing this before. He kicked Sarah's back door in. *Yes, I remember this.* Damien stood there casting a death spell on Sarah. Salvator holding her friend back. *What is going on? Am I dreaming?* Darkness. *Oh god, please stop the pain.* He could hear voices again…only this time it wasn't chaotic screaming and crying, more like fast paced matter of fact voices. *What's going on? It's so dark. Ooouuuucccchh. Please stop the pain. I can't catch my breath. Why is it so dark? Can't anyone hear me? Sarah? Sophia? Where are you Sarah?*

It's so dark. *Am I dead? No, no I can't be. Who is that talking? I have to find Sarah. I need to find her. Am I walking? It's so dark....wait is that light? It is ...*

"Luke stay with me, don't you die!"

Sarah? But it's so dark, "SARAH!" Luke's mind was yelling. It sounded like her voice but the voice was so faint, so far away, and the light up ahead is so inviting. Luke felt torn in what way to go. Follow the light or Sarah's voice. The light had a stronger pull on him. There was another voice he could hear, it too was faint but getting louder the closer he got to the light. Luke could barely hear Sarah's beautiful voice. The brightness of the light was almost too bright. It hurt Luke's eyes. His eyes widen.

It was as if his life was replaying and he was the only one invited to the movie. It was him as a kid. He tried turning and going back to Sarah's voice but couldn't, it was as if he was suppose to follow the kid him. So he did. He was hoping it would lead him back to Sarah.

He was walking home from school, it was raining and he was soaked. He remembered it as if it was yesterday...

It was so cold out and he was wet from the down pour the April showers brought. He hated the walk from school to home but he loved walking in to his warm house and into the arms of his loving mother, who faithfully waited for him to come home. On the coldest of days he just had to feel her arms wrapped around him and he was instantly warm all the way to the core of his body. He loved her. He was the youngest of four children and the only boy, but even so he knew he was his mother's favorite, she told him so.

His father on the other hand was quite opposite of his mother. He always came home in the evening and always grumpy. The children stayed together in their rooms or at least on the opposite side of the house from him. Luke noticed that his father seemed to be angrier towards him then his sisters and when he asked his mother why, his mother only excused the behavior with 'he had a lot on his mind' and 'one day he might understand'. The only thing he understood was to not understand how someone so loving as his mom would end up with someone so full of anger and mean. He wondered what she saw in him, saw past his anger and unkind attitude or did he treat her differently when kids weren't around. What he didn't know is that later on in his own life, he would understand what was going on with his fathers.

There were rules in the house and the children obeyed them. They were afraid of their father. The girls helped their mother with inside chores and Luke helped his dad with the outside ones. The children had to mind their manners and be respectful of their elders and they did their homework and chores before playing and under no circumstance were they to play in the attic.

When he asked once about the attic and questioned why they couldn't go in it, his dad slapped him for even asking. He never asked again. Although there was an occasional dare to go in the attic by his sisters, he never forgot the slap so he never fell for it.

As he got older the bond between him and his mother grew while the one with his father diminished completely. He was filling out in his own skin, now standing taller than his mother. He had tried many times to build a bond with his father; after all he was a boy and wanted his father's approval but unsuccessfully. It broke his mother's heart to see it happening over the years but kept the heartache to herself. Except for the few times she confronted his father on it but that always turned into a big fight so his mother stopped trying too.

The two older sisters married as soon as they graduated high school. They felt it was their only way out of the house. They hated the way their father treated them, so without looking back, they left. The third daughter was a junior in high school and already talking about doing a college abroad. She want to go to the United States. She would sit up late into the night, when Luke would crawl into bed with her because of another bad nightmare, and tell him stories of the U.S. She made it sound so great. She already knew what state and college she would go to. He thought maybe one day he would be able to join her, if for nothing else to get away from their father.

The time came and his last sister left home. She did exactly what she said she would do. She left for the United States on a student visa. He cried in his room that night. He would miss her terribly. It was only him and his parents, what would he do now. He spent most of his evenings hiding out in his room once his father came home. His father always returned after dinner, even though his mom would keep a plate warm for him, and have had a few drinks. Most people Luke had seen with alcohol in them became happy, even the grumpiest of them, but not his father, it made him even worse. Luke wanted to know more then ever what his father's problem was with him but out of respect never asked. Sensing the tension coming to a head, he asked his mother if he could go spend the summer with his grandparents. They were on the opposite side of the Fruili district. Not too far from his mother but far enough away from his father. His mother agreed.

It was the first day of summer, 1990, and Luke was 15 years old. He was a little worried leaving his mother all alone but she urged him to go, that maybe her and his father could use the time to reconnect. That put him to some ease. He was looking forward to seeing his grandparents. The bus ride was long, at least from a 15 year olds mind. He was glad to be away from his house. It was his 1st trip away from home alone.

He arrived at the bus station in the evening to find his grandparents waiting for him. It had been a long time since he had seen them last. He stood there examining their faces. He didn't remember them looking so old but again it had been about 10 years. He suddenly felt hate towards his father for cutting ties with them all those years ago. His grandparents looked so fragile now. He had missed them so. His grandmother had wept at the sight of him. She remembered a little boy and standing in front of her now stood the starts of a man, one that already towered over her. She could feel his strength when he hugged her. She had missed him. *Its going to be a great summer,* she thought.

They arrived back to the house. He was in awe of it. The house was beautiful. His grandmother had a meal already prepared for him. She knew he would be hungry from the bus ride. He was indeed. They sat at the table with him as he ate. He went back for seconds and then thirds. They laughed as they watched him eat. It was nice to see a youngster in the house again.

"Don't they feed you at home?" His grandfather teased as he laughed. His grandmother was laughing too. He couldn't help but join in on the laughter. It had to have been a sight watching him shove three plates of food into his mouth.

After dinner he took a little tour of the house. It was so warm and inviting, so different then his own. Like his father, he wondered what his grand father did for a living but knew not to ask. They sat outside in the warm air overlooking the lake behind the house. The view was very pretty. His grandparents asked about his likes and dislikes, if there was a girl he liked, sports, his sisters and even his mother but what they didn't ask about was his father and he was glad about that.

It had been a long day for Luke and he was tired. He said good night to his grandparents and retired to what would be his room for the next couple of months. He laid down on the bed and listened to the new sounds that surrounded him. He was at peace.

The next morning he woke to the smells of food..*yumm*. To his surprise, he was hungry. He got dressed and went into the kitchen to find his grandmother waiting for him with a table full of food.

"Wow grams that's a lot of food!" letting out a little smirk.

"Well you can eat a lot of food!" she said as they sat and laughed.

"Where's Grandfather?"

"He went to town. He will be back this evening. Say I was wondering if you would like to go to town with me today? Introduce you to a few people." She said with anticipation.

"Absolutely Grams!" he said as he started to shovel the food into his mouth.

"Slow down boy, we have time." She laughed.

The ride into town was nice, Theresa thought as she got to know her grandson again. It had been way too long. They chatted more about his life and what his interests were. She tested him by asking questions that were already asked the night before but she wanted to see if he was telling everything or not. His grandmother asked how things were at home. Luke's smile left his face.

"Is it that bad?" She asked with concern in her voice.

"I just don't know why he hates us all so much grams."

She could hear the pain in his voice and she didn't want him sad, it hurt her to see the pain in his eyes. She reached over and patted his leg.

"It's ok honey. You're here with us and we will have a great time. No more sadness, ok?"

"Ok," he said giving his grandmother a half grin and turned his head and looked out his window, trying to shake off the pain. They pulled up to a little café. He looked over at his grandmother.

"This is where I meet up with my friends. We have our coffee and chat a bit. It's a good start to the day."

He didn't mind. It made him feel good. He felt like he belonged. He loved his mother and she did try hard to make up for the lack of love from his dad, but she never went anywhere. She seemed to have only a couple of friends, and they always came to the house to visit. He wondered if his father had something to do with that. He never asked, it wasn't proper for a child to get involved in adult things. It did seem that his grandparents had a very loving relationship. He saw them holding hands the night before out on the patio. He had never seen his parents do that.

Luke enjoyed sitting with his grandmother and her friends. He learned a lot about the kind of person his grandmother was from the stories her friends were telling him. The visit went by quick.

"Grandmother, will I be able to come back with you again to visit with your friends?"

"Absolutely honey," She said in her usual soft voice.

She drove him around the town so Luke could see some of the sights. They made stops at the grocery store, the farmers market for fresh vegetables and then to the art gallery and the museum. He was impressed at the knowledge she had about the town and its past.

The time flew by and it was time to get back to the house to start dinner. Luke helped with what he could and watched his grandmother when he couldn't. He liked being around her. It was peaceful and for the first time in a really long time he felt calm.

That evening when his grandfather came home they sat down at the dining room table and had dinner together, talking and laughing. That was new to Luke and he loved it.

That night it came again, his nightmare. He felt fear and darkness. He was somewhere very dark but he seemed to know where to go, *strange*, he thought. He felt like he was floating. Anger and rage filled his entire body. *What's going on?* He could hear grumbling coming from his own mouth. He didn't like how this all felt. He felt out of breath, out of control. *Why was this happening? Is that a foot of a bed I see in the darkness?*

He woke up coughing. He must have

been loud because his grandfather was sitting on the side of his bed trying to shake him awake.

"Son, wake up. Are you ok?"

"Yes grandfather, I'm fine. It was just a nightmare."

"A nightmare? What was it about?" that caught his grandfather's attention. *No! Not this soon.*

"I can't remember the specifics gramps," Luke lied. He remembered every detail but didn't want to worry him.

"Are you ok?" he asked with worry in his voice.

"Yes, again I am fine."

"Ok, ok. Just making sure," he tucked his grandson back in and headed for the door, pausing a moment in the door way to look back at his grandson, who looked well on his way back into a deep sleep. *He's gotten so big, on the verge of being a man,* he thought with sadness. Antonio went back to his room.

"Is everything ok with Luke?" his wife asked.

"Its started," he said as he crawled back into bed.

"Oh no!" Theresa gasped, "does he know?"

"I don't think so. He seems to think it's

just bad dreams."

"Should we call his parents?"

"No, not yet, don't need to alarm them, not the way Anthony is. It could send him over the edge."

"Ok, but we are going to have to watch him closely."

"Yes, and we will be there to help him. He will be confused," he said.

"We have to make sure he doesn't become angry and withdrawn like his father. I thank every day that it skipped you," she said with a kiss to his cheek.

"Me to Bella. Me to."

The rest of the night was quiet from nightmares. In the morning Luke found both his grandparents at the table, and again the table was full of food. *How does she know I was going to be so hungry*, he thought smiling.

"How are you doing this morning?" his grandfather asked with questioning eyes.

"A little tired, a lot hungry, otherwise good," Luke said with a smile, "I'm good, but sorry I woke you."

"Don't you worry about that son. I just worried about you."

"No need to be, I have gotten use to them."

"Have them a lot?" His grandmother quizzed anxiously.

"I do but as of the past year or so, more then before."

"Have you told your parents?"

"No. I stay away from dad as much as I can."

"And your mother?"

"I don't want to burden her with my silly nightmares."

"Is it that bad there?" his grandfather asked.

"Yes, I don't understand why dad treats us so bad. It has driven my sisters away and honestly I can't wait to leave myself," Luke said. He hated feeling like that. He loved his mother; he just couldn't deal with his dad's bad attitude.

His grandparents knew not to push and they could see that it bothered him to talk about it so they changed the subject.

"So today we thought we would show you some of the country side, venture out a little, if you wanted." His grandfather said.

"Sounds good gramps. When do we leave?"

"Gramps? Hmm," his grandfather said with a chuckle. Theresa laughed at her husband who clearly wasn't up on today's youth's vocabulary.

"We will leave after you two help me clean up this breakfast mess," Luke's grandmother said smiling. *Having Luke there made the house feel alive again* she thought.

It was a sunny, warm summer day. He loved the scenery. They all sat in silence for some time and then his grandmother started talking about things they were passing. She seemed to have a story for everything. It made Luke smile. Luke's grandparents knew where they were heading and in hopes that it would look familiar to Luke, at least from the stand point of his nightmares.

He watched as his grandfather grabbed his wife's hand to hold it. They would take turns glancing at each other and smiling. *They really must love each other,* Luke noted.

They pulled up to a huge wrought iron gate and Luke watched as the gate slowly opened when the car inched towards it. *It was like magic. Like it knew we were there, how cool,* Luke thought. He saw the castle that was beyond the gate. He was mesmerized by it as the car slowly rolled closer to it.

"Where are we?" Luke asked.

"You'll see," his grandmother replied.

His grandfather knocked on the door and the door slowly creaked open. They were instructed to come in by what Luke could only assume to be a butler by the way he was dressed.

"Wow, how cool," he whispered to his grandmother. The inside was cold with a dark and creepy appearance. Luke found himself reaching out to hold his grandmother's hand. She gave out a little chuckle.

"It's ok, don't be afraid," she said.

"It seems spookier then it really is, you'll see." Her calm demeanor made him feel calm. *If she said so then it must be so*, he thought. But he wasn't going to let go of his grandmother's hand, just in case. She didn't mind. She knew he would need someone to lean on.

They were taken down a dimly lit hall and he could see light coming from the room at the end of the cold stoned hallway. This was his first time in a castle. He was in awe and creeped out at the same time. They entered into a large study and the books went from ceiling to floor on every wall except the wall where there was a huge rock fireplace with a fire burning in it. There was a sitting area with maroon leather couches facing each other and two oversized arm chairs on each end and a marble coffee table in the middle with magazines fanned out in the center. Even though the room was so big, the books, the fire, the colors made it feel warm and cozy.

The butler went over to the arm chair that faced away from them and spoke to someone sitting in it. The butler then motioned Luke and his grandparents to sit down on one of the couches. Theresa could feel her grandson's hand tighten around hers. She worried how he was going to deal with what was coming, seeing how bad Anthony dealt with it.

Antonio sat first and closest to the arm chair, then Luke was instructed to sit next by his grandfather and then his grandmother sat down last. Luke looked toward the chair and felt his eyes widen. There sat the oldest man he had ever seen with a blanket on his lap and one around his shoulders. His grandmother nudged him to let him know not to stare, he quickly looked away.

"It's been a long time my friend." The old man spoke in a soft worn down voice to Antonio.

"It has," his grandfather not excited about seeing him.

"So who is this fine looking young fellow?" the old man asked already knowing the answer.

"This is my grandson Luke, Anthony's boy," his grandfather going along with the charade to not alert Luke this meeting was because of him.

The old man's eyes sparkled with finally meeting the boy.

"Really? That's wonderful," the old man said, looking more sinister then ever. "Does he…"

"No, but close," Antonio cut him off with a shake of his head.

"Nightmares?"

"Yes."

Luke sat there puzzled as to why they

were talking about him. He glanced at his grandmother who just smiled back at him. The old man named Damien scared him a little. He thought Damien was creepy especially how he kept staring at him. *What's going on*, he wondered but knew not to speak until told too.

Chapter 14

The visit seemed long for Luke, but as long as his grandmother was there he didn't mind. He didn't like the fact that the creepy old man and his grandfather were talking in a weird way to each other about him. Once they left the creepy castle his grandfather spoke.

"Son, I know you must be wondering what that was all about. Unfortunately right now, I can't say but you will understand soon."

Luke just nodded ok. He didn't know if he wanted to know, especially if it involved that old man. They drove further away from town; the scenery didn't seem to change, rolling hills of grapes from the vineyards, open country sides and an occasional farm house.

"Where are we going?" Luke asked.

"Your grandmother and I thought that seen is how you're becoming a man that you should look like one so we are going into Venice and while we are there we thought about a nice dinner out."

"Really? Cool," Luke was surprised. His father and mother never did this with him or his sisters. His mom always brought home clothes from second hand stores and mended or dyed them to make them look new. Luke hated it.

They took him to a real tailor. He was in shock. He thought tailors were for wealthy people only and his parents were far from that. At least that's what his parents wanted him to believe. He was fitted for an entire wardrobe which included two suits. His grandparents also took him to the shoe store and he was fitted for a new pair of dress shoes. He couldn't stop smiling. He felt like he was an important person the way he was being waited on. It made his grandparents happy to see Luke so happy. They would do what they had to do to keep him from going down the same dark road their only son had gone down.

Luke didn't realize that this summer would change him; everything about him. He looked over at his grandparents and wished that they could always be around. He loved how they treated him and loved watching how they were with each other. He felt good inside. He could see his grandmother weeping.

"Grandmother, are you ok?"

"Yes honey I am. You're just getting so big."

"Ok grams," old people are so sentimental Luke thought as he said that. His grandfather patted him on the back as to say it was ok.

They went to the fanciest restaurant Luke had ever seen. When the waiter came over to the table he treated Luke like he too was an adult and Luke liked that. This experience would mold him into the man he would become and he would become accustomed to the fancy restaurants, expensive clothes, fast cars and being treated like he was made of gold. It was dark when they left the restaurant and would be very late by the time they returned home.

"Thank you grandfather and grandmother for the best day of my life and for the clothes," Luke said with a sleepy voice.

"Your welcome son," his grandfather said as he helped his half asleep grandchild into bed.

"Get some rest," his grandmother said as she kissed his forehead.

"Ok," Luke said quietly as he shut his eyes.

The next few days he spent with his grandmother in the garden and going to town to visit her friends. He looked forward to each day with his grandparents. When the weekend came around he went with his grandfather to the creepy castle. He sat and listened to his grandfather and the old man Damien talk in code about him. He started to look around at all the books. There were so many of them. He noticed some really old ones high up on the shelves and asked if he could use the ladder that was attached to the wall that slid back and forth. Damien said he could.

His grandfather and Damien knew that to

Luke it would seem like stories he would read out of the old books, but the stories were more then that. They were the key to the past and to Luke's future. The men also knew that Luke had to figure out that what he thought were nightmares were not. They had to wait until he pieced it all together. They knew it would be soon. They left him alone as he read the books. They figured the more he read the sooner he would piece it together and understand which meant the sooner they could help. Until then they had to be patient.

After a few weekends he started to like going to the old dark castle. He liked reading the stories of the witches in Italy and Sicily. He didn't tell his grandparents but the stories gave him nightmares, but he couldn't stop reading. He wanted to know more and wanted to know what happened to the witches.

"Damien did you write these books?" Luke asked one day as he studied the covers and saw what he thought was Damien's name hand written in the back of one.

"No," was all Damien could say. He couldn't say anymore. He knew he was bound by the way of their kind.

"He has to be having nightmares, but he hasn't said anything," Antonio whispered to Damien.

"Would have been nice to count on his father," Damien snarled.

"Yeah not sure why he won't, guess he is just to angry." They sat there watching Luke emerge himself in to the books.

It was about half way through Luke's summer when his grandmother received a call one sunny warm day. They had just finished with lunch and were clearing the table. The glass slipped from her hand crashing down on the tiled kitchen floor below. It made Luke jump. He didn't know it then but he would end up reliving that exact moment over and over in his mind. His grandmother's voice went from happy to a low whisper. Luke could see sadness wash over her face. She hung up the phone.

"Grandma, are you ok?" Luke asked as he got up and started to help his grandmother pick up the broken glass. She went over and got the broom out of the pantry and swept up the rest.

"Grandma, are you ok?" he asked again. She was crying.

"Grams?" he said in a soft voice.

"Honey you need to go into the other room please," she said choking back the tears as she picked up the phone and dialed a number.

"You need to come home now," she said and then hung up the phone and sat back down at the table and waited, weeping into her hands.

Luke stood in the doorway of the kitchen watching his grandmother. He didn't think she even saw him there, he thought. It hurt him to see her crying. He heard a car come to a screeching halt in the driveway. The door flung open, his grandfather flew in slamming the door shut and even though Luke was watching the whole thing it still made him jump.

"What's going on?" he said in a deep, low voice as he reached his wife.

"Sit down, I have to tell you something," She said in a distraught voice. Seeing his wife's face, he sat down and put his hands on hers.

"What's wrong?" he asked with worry in his voice.

"Marie called," She started to say. His grandfather looked in Luke's direction and his grandmother looked over as well.

"Go in the other room Luke please," she said again in a soft crackling voice. Luke stood against the wall in the other room so he could still hear his grandparents.

"What's going on? Does he have to go back?" he asked in a panicked voice. He wasn't ready to have his grandson go back. "Maybe I can call and talk to them," he had continued, but his wife cut him off.

"No, yes….yes he does, he's gone. He's dead," she started crying.

"Who's gone? Who's dead?" he questioned as he grabbed his wife's hands and pulled them away from her face.

"Anthony," she could barely choke out his name.

"No!" Luke shouted out as he slid down

the wall and buried his face into his knees and started crying.

Luke's grandparents looked at each other when they heard Luke and got up when they heard the thud coming from the other room. They found him with his head in his knees.

"Oh honey I'm sorry," his grandmother said trying to mask her own pain in her voice, as she bent down and hugged him. He wrapped his arms around her neck and sobbed on her shoulder. His grandfather sat down beside him and put his hand on Luke's back and quietly sobbed as well.

They all had the same thought. They had all wished to have had a better relationship with him. They had all wished he didn't pass being so angry, but most of all Luke wished he had the kind of relationship that he and his grandfather had with his father. Instead of sending him on the bus, Luke's grandparents decided to drive him home. Luke liked that. He didn't want to be away from them. He needed them now more then ever.

It was a long and quiet ride home. Luke's eyes were all puffed up from the crying he had done and the lack of sleep over the course of the ride. When they arrived at Luke's house they saw quite a few cars. Luke drug his feet getting inside. He didn't want to be there. Seeing his mother in so much pain was unbearable. He hated seeing her in pain. His two older sisters brought their husbands and hung to them for support so he was happy he had Sophia, she was his favorite. He had been so lonely when she left home. Luke hated the feeling the house had always given him. It was always dark and gloomy but now sadness was added to that list. He hated being there.

He choked back the tears as he watched his father's casket being lowered. The preacher was talking but all he could hear was crying from family and friends that sat and stood around him.

It was too hot to be wearing a suit, he was messing with his collar, and he couldn't breath. *Darn collar*, he thought. He wanted to leave. *When is this going to get over?* He looked at his mother, then at his grandparents. The preacher walked over and told him that he was now the man of the house. He didn't want to be. He was just a kid. His childhood, as of that moment, was over.

When everyone had left, the house seemed to have a darkness that loomed in it. It was a quiet eerie darkness. His grandparents stayed about a week and there was a lot of talk between them and Luke's mother. He wondered if it was about him. They seem to become quiet when he entered the room. He didn't question why. He hated to see his grandparents go but they told him he could come see them anytime he wanted.

About a week after his grandparents left, his sister had to go back to the United States. She told him to come and see her soon. He agreed that he would.

His mother was a mess and it was always dark and quiet in the house. She didn't want to leave the house and most of the time just laid in bed crying, longing for her husband. She feared for her son, that he would suffer the same fate if he doesn't have the proper frame of mind to deal with what his father had too. She didn't want her son to suffer as he had. She knew she had to put her suffering aside to be a better support for him. She owed him that much.

Before he knew it school had started up again. He didn't have any interest in school, not this year. He used to love school, it got him out of the house and away from his father and now he just wanted to be with his grandparents. He missed being there more then ever.

His nightmares were becoming more and more often. He figured it was because of his father dying but the nightmares were not of him. He didn't understand. He called his grandparents often and told his grandmother about them.

"Have you told you mother?"

"No, I haven't, she is so sad. I don't want to worry her," he said.

"I understand. Are you helping her out?" his grandmother asked.

"I'm trying. I miss being there with you and grandfather."

"I know honey and I know it's tough for you right now," She said with a sympathetic voice.

Luke could feel his eyes fill with tears.

"Stay strong son and know that anytime you need to talk, your grandfather and I are here for you," she added.

"I know."

"Maybe we can come down and visit again soon."

"I would like that," Luke said quietly.

"Ok honey, you keep your chin up and stay strong."

"Ok grams," Luke said.

"Love you Luke."

"Love you grams," and with that Luke hung up.

Everything Luke was going through was changing him. He was becoming withdrawn at school and dark. He started to fancy the darker colors of things and the nightmares were invading his thoughts.

The thoughts were dark and creepy. In his nightmares he would find himself standing over people or in people's rooms, but he seems to not be able to touch them. He seemed to be restricted in a way. He could only move back and forth at the foot of their beds. He soon realized it would be people who he was mad at or people who did bad things to him.

When his grandparents came to visit he cornered his grandfather. He was hoping he wasn't going crazy and needed a man to talk too.

"Grandfather, Can we talk?"

"Sure son, what's going on?"

"It's my nightmares," Luke said quietly.

"Oh? What's wrong?" his grandfather asked with a concerned look on his face, but already knew what Luke was going to say.

"In the nightmares I'm standing at the foot of people's beds, but not just any people, ones that have made me angry or have hurt my feelings."

It's about time, his grandfather thought. His concerned face masking the excitement that it was almost time. "Anything else?"

"No, I have tried going beyond the foot of the beds but can't. It's like I'm being blocked."

"Hmm," his grandfather said.

"Am I going crazy?"

"No son, your not. I think that it's time for you to come back with your grandmother and I."

"What about mom?"

"She will come too."

"Ok. Just didn't want her left alone."

"You're shaping up to becoming a fine young man."

Luke smiled. *Good*, he thought. He

wanted to go back so bad but worried about his mother. She wasn't doing very well; he hoped the change of scenery would help. His mother didn't argue. She was actually very happy to get out of the house and away from town.

They left on a Friday night after Luke was out of school. On Sunday Luke and his grandfather went to see Damien. Luke didn't mind. He was actually looking forward to it so he could pick up where he had left off in the books. He enjoyed reading about the witches and the struggle between the good and bad witches and the witch hunts. He could picture the battles that took place. *Even if it was all make belief*, he thought. He would soon learn how wrong he was.

While they were at the castle, his grandmother took his mother out. They went to the café and met her friends; they went to the farmers market and walked around the town. Theresa wanted Marie to get out and live life. She saw that Marie was closing herself off more then she already had over the years and she felt bad. Marie use to be so full of life but after she married her son and dealing with her son's behavior, it ran Marie down. They talked about Luke and what he was starting to go through.

Theresa reassured Marie that they were going to be there for Luke so he wouldn't turn out like his father, so bitter and angry. Marie hoped and prayed for that not to happen. She had already lost her husband; she didn't want to lose her son too. Theresa reassured her again.

"When do they normally get back when they go to the castle?' Marie asked.

"It's usually an all day trip, but with Luke being so close to knowing it could be longer," Theresa responded.

Marie was saddened by this, she was hoping her son would have been one the curse skipped, but it didn't and she had hoped his grandparents and Damien could help him before he shuts himself off like his father had.

Chapter 15

The stories were the coolest Luke had ever read. He gets into reading them so much so that he forgets that he is in the castle with the creepy old man watching his every move.

"The boy needs to stay here for a few days," Damien said in a cold to-the-point manner.

"I'm not sure he would feel comfortable enough yet to stay," Antonio said defensively, "especially seen is how he just lost his father."

"He needs to stay soon," Damien said sharply and started to say something else but Antonio cut him off.

"I will work on that," Antonio turned his attention to Luke. "Luke, it's time to go," breaking Luke's concentration on the books.

"Already?" He asked.

"Yes. Your mother and grandmother are waiting. We'll come back again soon," as he shot a glare over at Damien.

"Ok," Luke said as he put the books away and thanked Damien.

"You're welcome Luke. See you soon," Damien said. The butler walked them out. Antonio sat in his car staring at the castle for a moment.

"Grandfather what it is?" Luke asked.

"Oh, ah nothing."

Luke didn't buy it. Something was going on. He could feel tension between the old man and his grandfather, but Luke knew it would be disrespectful if he pushed. His grandfather started the car and pulled out.

"Keep an eye on him as well. Something isn't sitting well with me. There's something going on with Antonio," Damien instructed his butler.

"Will do sir," the butler responded. He has been Damien's right hand man for many, many years, like his father before him and the father before that. He knew Damien's past and his secrets and also knew not to cross Damien. A loyal servant he was.

When Luke and Antonio returned home, Luke's mother wrapped her arms around her boy.

"Mother, too tight," Luke gasped barely able to breath.

"Oh sorry," she said giving him a smile.

"How was the visit?" his grandmother asked.

"It was good," Luke said.

His grandfather shot a look over at his wife. She knew then that there was something wrong. They both snuck off to their room, leaving Luke and his mother to chat about the day they each had.

"What is it?" Theresa asked Antonio with a nervous tone.

"I think there is something Damien is hiding and he is becoming relentless about Luke staying with him. It concerns me," he answered.

"I remember when Anthony stayed with him. That's around the time he became withdrawn and angry." Knowing her husband she added, "What are you going to do?"

"Well I will continue taking him as often as I had been but watch Damien closer and I don't trust that butler of his either."

"Just be careful honey," she knew not to tell him that she didn't want them going. He is the man of the house after all.

"I will Bella," as he gave her a kiss on her forehead.

They went back out to the living room to check on Luke and Marie, finding them sitting together on the couch talking about the stories

Luke had been reading.

"Say I was thinking, why don't you move in here with us. Family has to stick together and it would be good for you two to get a fresh start and this place is definitely big enough for all of us," Antonio said with a pleading voice. That made Luke very happy.

"I don't know, we don't need to turn your lives upside down," Luke's mother said.

"Oh come on mom! PLEASE?" Luke begged.

"It would be great!" Theresa added.

"Well, Luke what about school and your friends?" his mother asked.

"School is school, and I will make new friends," Luke said still pleading.

"Ok, ok. Guess I'm out numbered," his mother replied defeated.

"Thank you," Luke said practically jumping into his mother's arms hugging her. It made her laugh. Antonio and Theresa looked at each other and smiled. It had been a long time since Marie laughed.

"Great it's settled, we will leave tomorrow and pack everything up and get back here and get you two settled into your new lives."

"That soon?" Marie asked.

"The sooner the better," he said back, giving her a look. She caught on.

"Ok, suppose your right," she said.

Luke was so excited. He couldn't sleep that night and he didn't care, just meant no nightmares, but by morning he was exhausted. He slept most of the ride home snuggled against his mother in the back seat of his grandparent's car. His grandfather had a little trailer attached to the back of the car, so not much would be coming back.

They would be staying just long enough to pack what they needed and sale the rest. Marie put the house up for sale and gave the realtor hers, Antonio's and Theresa's cell numbers. A lifetime was spent in that house and it showed by all the stuff in it. Luke watched his grandfather and mother put a very old chest in the trailer.

"What's that?" Luke asked with inquisitive eyes.

"Oh this? Something that has been passed down through the generations and one day will be yours," his grandfather explained.

"What's in it?"

"Well when you get it, then you get to know."

"When do I get it?"

"When you're all grown up."

"I have to wait that long?"

"I'm afraid so."

"That stinks," Luke huffed as he threw a big bag into the trailer. His grandfather laughed at the frustration his grandson's face was showing.

Marie was in her bedroom taking her time packing up her things. It made her weepy having to decide what stayed and what went. She was about done in the closet when she ran her hand along the shelf high above her. She had to stand on a little foot stool. Her fingertips felt something different towards the corner of the shelf. *Hmmm, what is that*, she thought. She stood on her tippy toes and managed to barely grab it. It was a little box. She took it over to the bed and she sat down, dumping the contents out on the bed beside her. She hadn't seen these very old pieces in a very long time. The box belonged to her late husband and he only told her it was something he had to keep and had to pass it down to Luke when he became a man. She tried to find out more in the beginning of their marriage but with no luck in getting answers, so she left it alone, seeing how angry Anthony would get. She let out a big sigh and wiped the tears from her cheeks. As she put the contents back into the box, she noticed a folder jammed in the bottom. She hadn't remembered seeing it before. She pulled it out and opened it. She saw that her late husband had in fact been looking for an ancestor to break the curse. He never told her. She quickly glanced through it, knowing she needed to get it put away before Luke came in. She put the contents back into the box and stuck it on her dresser. She grabbed the folder off the bed and went out to the trailer where Antonio was rearranging it.

"Look what I found," Marie said to Antonio as she passed the folder to him as she looking around to make sure Luke wasn't near. Antonio opened it up and did a quick once over.

"Hmm. Interesting," is all he said as he stuck it under the driver seat of the car. Marie knew he would know what to do with it. She didn't tell him about the box. She went back inside the house to her room and grabbed the box off the dresser. She found a piece of paper and wrote her daughter a short letter.

My precious Sophia,

I am sending you this box for you to put up for safe keeping. As you know, Luke and I are moving in with your grandparents and need for you to hang on to this box for me. There will come a point where I will ask for it back. Please don't question me about the contents and please never open the box or ask around about it either. I know I'm asking you for a lot but it truly is for your own safety that you don't know.

Love always,
Your mother

Marie taped up the box and then put the letter in an envelope and addressed it to her daughter and taped it to the box. She had the box in one arm and picked up the last bag of clothes with her free hand as she glanced around the room one last time. *Good bye Anthony*, she thought as she turned and left.

She put the box in the back seat where she would sit and Antonio took the bag from her and stuck it in the trailer; it was the last thing that would fit. He strapped down the trailer with a tarp. They were ready to go but had to wait on the antique dealer to show up. He was going to purchase the furniture from her at a great price. It would be enough money to hold her over with until she could find a job.

Marie locked up the house one last time and turned the keys over to the realtor. She stood in the walkway staring at the house. It was a bittersweet good bye. She will miss her home. She had lived there her whole adult life but she was also looking forward to a new life in a new place, if it meant helping her son. Before setting out for the long ride back, she had Antonio stop by the post office to mail the package.

On the ride back Marie knew that like her son's, her life had changed so much already and hoped that this journey would prove to be a good move for the two of them. She worried about her son so much and wondered if his life would turn out like his father. She swore to herself in that car that she would do whatever she had to, to make sure her son was safe and to grow up having a good life. She had heard stories of how Damien was but never seen him for herself and from what she was told, she didn't want to either.

When they arrived back in Udine it was very late. Marie put Luke to bed and helped unpack the trailer. She and Antonio put the chest up in the attic. They figured the sooner it was put away the better. It wouldn't bring up any more questions from Luke. Antonio took the folder out of the car and stuck it in a desk drawer in his study. He figured that was a good spot because he knew Luke knew the desk was off limits to him. He was curious as to what his son was up to before he died. It was a peaceful night in the house. No nightmares for Luke, at lease not on this night.

Over the course of the next few weeks they all got settled in living together and getting a schedule down. For the first ever in her life Marie got a part time job as a waitress at the small café that Theresa meets up with her friends. Marie was grateful to Theresa for helping her get the job. She loved the idea of the independence it would bring. She liked the café. It seemed to be the one in which the older crowd came to. Marie seemed to be accepted immediately and her customers loved her. She was very sweet and soft spoken they would say to Theresa.

Luke settled in at the local school and he didn't really care that he was the new kid and that he didn't seem to fit in. He didn't have any interest in school anyway. He had other things going on in his life that were more pressing. He was in fact a loner.

A few months had passed and Antonio was getting ready to leave for the day when he opened his desk drawer while looking for something and saw the folder. He had meant to read it. He picked it up and took it with him. He had his own favorite place to go. He would hunker down at the local pub, not to drink but because no one bothers him there. He orders his usual, a black coffee and opened up the folder. He was shocked by how much his son had gotten done. He saw that his son had in fact found a living ancestor that could end the curse. She lived in the United States. He saw her age. She was as old as Luke; just a kid. *Is that why his son never did anything to end the curse is that why he became so tormented, so mean?* He asked himself. He would keep tabs on her and if need be pass the information on to Luke when he became an adult.

Just as Luke was getting use to not having his nightmares, it started back up. He would dream of a dark evil shadow that haunted his bedroom, or it would be of witches or of a girl about his age. A girl he had never seen before. His dreams use to scare him but now the only one that still did was of the dark thing. It had such an evil presence about it; Luke knew to be scared of it but didn't know the reason as to why. He figured the dreams of the witches were because of the books he read and he was drawn to the girl but didn't know why and he didn't care really, she was nice to dream about. He would find out in adulthood who she was, he would know her in his adult life; she would be the key to it all.

"Hello?" Antonio said as he answered the phone one evening.

"Why haven't you been here?" Damien asked in a short angry tone.

"Been busy," Antonio snapped back with an even shorter tone.

"Bring the boy here," Damien demanded.

"This weekend!"

"Don't keep me waiting, be here, don't make me send for you," Damien said in a threatening voice.

"I said we'll be there. Save your threats for someone it would actually work on," Antonio said as he hung the phone up. He hadn't realized that his wife was standing behind him in the doorway.

"What was that about?" she asked with a worried look on her face.

"It was Damien, and he is getting upset that I haven't brought Luke over in such a long time."

"Why haven't you?"

"Marie found a folder when she was packing to come here. I had forgotten about it until recent and I finally took a look at it. Anthony had been searching for someone to break the curse and he succeeded."

"That's great!" Theresa said with a smile.

"No, it's a little girl about Luke's age."

"Oh," she said as her smile faded. She let out a little sigh as Antonio pulled her in close to him and wrapped his arms around her.

"I think something more is going on with Damien and it worries me," he said.

"What do you mean?" she asked breaking his hold and looking directly into his eyes.

"I'm not sure what it is but the last time we were there, Damien was so adamant about Luke staying there and the way he was acting made me nervous. Something wasn't right. I have to figure it out and soon."

"Please be careful, we don't know to the extent of what Damien is capable of."

"I will be," he said as he pulled his wife back into his arms. He said that to comfort her but the truth was he is worried what Damien could and would do. They got their composure and went out to join Marie and Luke on the patio. It was still very warm considering the time of year.

"Luke how would you like to go visit Damien on Sunday?" his grandfather asked.

"Really? Ok. I want to finish reading the books," Luke said.

"Yeah and then you can finish telling me about the witches," his mother said.

"Ok deal," Luke figured with a big smile.

"We will leave first thing Sunday morning," his grandfather said wearily.

For Antonio Sunday came too fast. He wasn't ready to deal with whatever plan Damien had for his grandson and Antonio knew Damien well enough to know he was indeed up to something, he also knew that his grandson's nightmares were coming on more and more which meant he was ready to know the truth. He just prayed that the truth didn't affect him like it had his father. Antonio couldn't lose another boy, not to the likes of Damien and that awful curse.

"Theresa, I don't know if I can do this again," Antonio told his wife when they woke up.

"I know. I'm afraid for him too," Theresa said softly, "but you know what would happen if you don't."

"That I know," he said as he kissed his wife's forehead and rolled out of bed. She followed her husband into the bathroom. They always took their morning shower together, it's where they talked, laughed, cried, fooled around, the shower was their time, and they say it's what has kept their marriage going strong for all those years. Theresa made breakfast with Marie's help and they all sat down at the table to eat.

"How did you sleep Luke?" Antonio asked his grandson.

"Ok I guess," Luke said as he continued to shove food into his mouth.

"You guess?" Luke's mom asked with a worried tone.

"Yeah I had a nightmare, but other then that, I slept good."

"Why didn't you wake me?" his mother asked.

"Mom, I'm a big boy. It was just a weird nightmare," Luke said trying to sound like a grown man.

"So what was the nightmare about?" Antonio asked curious to know what "weird" meant.

"Well, I was floating, or walking on air and I was in this girl's room. It was weird, I didn't even know who she was," Luke said as he ate. *He didn't seem to be bothered by it now*, his mother thought. Antonio, Theresa and Marie all shot glances at each other. They knew it was time and it sadden them greatly.

It meant that Marie had to go pack a suitcase and put it in the car. She finished breakfast and excused herself to her room. She closed the door behind her and sat on the edge of her bed and pulled out a pen and paper from the nightstand and wrote her son a little note.

Dear son,
I just wanted to let you know how proud I am of you and no matter what, I will always love you and will always be here for you. You will go through something very soon that you may not understand but you will. I promise and when you do it will answer a lot of questions about your father. Keep your chin up and love in your heart. We will be here for you. You will be home soon. Please don't worry and don't be scared. I'm only a phone call away.
I love you Luke,
Mom

She hadn't noticed that she was crying until a tear dropped on the paper. She wiped her eyes and folded up the piece of paper and put it on top of her son's clothes and closed up the suitcase. She could hear her son in the kitchen with his grandmother. *Good*, she sighed as she snuck out to the car where Antonio was waiting for her with the trunk opened. She placed the suitcase in the trunk but couldn't let go of the handle.

"Marie it will be ok, he will be ok. He is much stronger then Anthony was at his age, and he has us to come home too."

"I know. It's just…. It's just, it's my boy," Marie said crying again.

"Marie, you need to stop crying and get composure. We don't need Luke asking why you're upset."

"Your right," she said wiping her eyes again. Antonio gave Marie a hug.

"Really, it will be ok and over soon. Trust me," he said with a smile.

"Ok."

"Now try and go back inside and act like nothing is wrong," Antonio instructed. Marie nodded and snuck back inside.

"Luke it's time to go," Antonio yelled.

"Ok grandfather, be right there," Luke yelled back.

A moment later, Luke walked into the living room where his grandparents were.

"Seen mom? I can't find her," Luke said worried.

"I'm right here," Marie answered as she entered the room behind her son.

"Mom!" Luke said as he turned and wrapped his arms around his mother's waist and squeezed tight.

"Oh," Marie breathed. It caught her off guard. Tears started to fill her eyes again and she looked at Antonio. He gave her the 'be strong' look and she stopped herself from crying.

"Ok it's time to go, kiss your mother and grandmother good bye," Antonio said to Luke. Luke did what he was told and they headed out. Theresa and Marie stood on the porch until they could no longer see the car, holding each other, both of them shedding tears. It was going to be a long week and they were both afraid of what it was going to be like. What Luke would be like when he returned.

Antonio kept looking over at Luke on the drive to the castle. Luke seemed unaware of his grandfather's distressed face. The drive there seemed fast for Antonio but for Luke it seemed to take forever. He was excited to be able to read more about the witches. He found himself not wanting to put the books down.

As they pulled up to the big wrought iron gates, the gate doors suddenly opened slowly and Luke smiled as he looked at his grandfather.

"What's wrong grandfather?"

"Umm nothing, it's nothing."

Luke didn't buy it, something was up and suddenly he got a real bad feeling. His grandfather parked the car and they got out. Antonio started walking to the back of the car.

"Grandfather, what are you doing?" Luke asked as he started to follow his grandfather.

"Just go to the door Luke. I'm right behind you," Antonio snapped. Luke was shocked by his grandfather's attitude change. Antonio saw how that affected Luke but thought that it was the best way, even though it was breaking his own heart.

Luke was about to knock when the door opened.

"Hi Salvator," Luke said. The butler gave Luke the creeps.

"Come in Mr. Luke," Salvator instructed. Antonio started to enter too when Salvator stopped him.

"Not you. It starts now!" Salvator said in a low growl. They both looked over at Luke but he seemed oblivious to the hatred between the two men.

"But Luke isn't ready to be left like this," Antonio barked back.

"He will deal," Salvator growled again grabbing the suitcase out of Antonio's hand, and promptly shut the door in Antonio's face. That enraged him and broke his heart at the same time. He didn't get to give Luke a proper goodbye. He could hear Luke yelling from behind the door. He was yelling for his grandfather, he sounded scared, Antonio thought. Antonio had to go, it was destroying him to hear Luke crying out for him.

Luke ran to the nearest window and started pounding on the window crying out for his grandfather but he couldn't hear him.

"Boy, cut that out, you're here for the next week or two, so stop. There's a lot you have to learn so come," Salvator said as he grabbed the back of Luke's neck and led him down the dimly lit hall to the study.

Luke hurt inside and he was scared. *What is going on? Why am I here?*, he thought.

"I want to go home," he whispered under his breath.

"If you don't do as you are told, then you will never go home again!" Salvator said purposely to scare Luke. It worked. Luke was terrified.

Luke could hear very faint chanting. *What is that?* He thought as he fought hard, really hard to open his eyes.

It was dark; there were lights but very dim lights. It was cold and musty. *Where am I,* he asked softly as he managed to open his eyes all the way and looked around.

"He's awake," a deep raspy voice said. Luke couldn't make it out and his eyes shut again and everything went dark.

Chapter 16

"Sarah?" Jenny asked softly watching her friend's eyes squinting open.

"Sarah? Can you hear me?" Jenny asked again.

Sarah slowly came around and very confused. "Jenny?" she whispered as she looked around, a hospital room. She looked down; she was in the bed with IV's coming out of her arm. She started to get up startled by what she saw.

"Sarah, its ok lay down. Please lay back. Calm down," Jenny said pleading with Sarah. Sarah complied.

"Don't you ever scare me like that again," Jenny snarled in an irritated voice.

"Sorry?" Sarah said confused, "What happened?"

"You don't remember?" Jenny asked as she looked behind her. Sarah followed her gaze. There beyond the bed stood Frank and Sophia and it hit her like a ton of bricks.

"Oh God!" Sarah said as she started sobbing. Jenny wrapped her arms around Sarah trying to comfort her. "What am I doing in this bed?" Sarah asked through the tears.

"You passed out and it's no wonder with all that's happened," Jenny barked again as she helped Sarah lay back down.

"Where's Luke?" Sarah asked as she looked at their expressions change.

"Frank, Sophia could you give us a few minutes?" Jenny asked.

"Yes, absolutely," Frank and Sophia both said at the same time. Jenny waited until the door shut all the way behind them before she looked at Sarah.

"Where's Luke?" Sarah demanded.

"Sarah relax or I'm NOT telling you."

"I know your keeping something from me, out with it!"

"Relax first or I'm not saying," Jenny was just as stubborn as Sarah.

"Ok, Ok," Sarah gave in knowing Jenny wouldn't budge. Sarah laid back, closed her eyes and took a few deep relaxing breaths. She slowly opened them and looked at Jenny. "Ok I'm calm."

"After you fainted Frank, Sophia and I told the police everything that had happened. They seemed satisfied with that, for now anyway. I came here and stayed with you and Frank stayed with Sophia." Jenny paused.

"What Jenny?" Sarah questioned getting impatient for answers.

"Sarah, Luke's surgery went well, the doctor told Sophia that the next 24 hours will tell a lot about his recovery but because of his blood loss it didn't look good for him. He told her to prepare for the worst," Jenny said cautiously afraid of how Sarah was going to respond to the news.

"NO!" Sarah cried out, "I want to see him."

"Sarah," Jenny whispered then let out a big sigh, "there's more."

"What?" Sarah said sharply through her tears.

Jenny took a deep breath and let it out slowly as she continued, "the doctor took Sophia back to see Luke this morning but.." She hesitated again not wanting to tell her the news.

"Dammit Jenny! What is it?" Sarah asked getting upset.

"Sarah, he's gone."

"What? NO! He can't be," Sarah said

sobbing uncontrollably as she rubbed her stomach thinking about the little life that is growing in it. His baby.

"Sarah?" Jenny asked as she tried to calm Sarah down.

"Sarah?" Jenny said louder.

"Sarah! He isn't dead gone, he is missing gone," Jenny yelled at Sarah. It startled Sarah but she snapped out of whatever trance she was in.

"What?"

"When Sophia and the doctor went into his room, he wasn't in it. He's gone. The hospital is swarming with police and it's on the news. They say kidnapped. The hospital is on lock down and there is an officer posted outside your room."

"WHAT?" Sarah was in shock and confused. "How long was I out for?"

"Over 24 hours."

"Oh God," she whispered. She couldn't grasp what had happened, what was happening, it all seemed so unreal.

"They think it was the two old men that broke in your home. No one here seems to have seen anything, which I find hard to believe."

"He's gone?" Sarah couldn't wrap her mind around it. *Knock Knock.* "Come in," Sarah yelled. A police officer came in and shut the door.

"Ma'am I don't mean to bother you but thought you should know what happened," the man in blue paused. Sarah nodded for him to continue. "It's about your neighbors, the Wilsons."

Sarah shot up into a sitting position, "What about them?" She could feel her heart starting to race again.

"Sarah calm down or I'll make him leave!" Jenny said in a stern voice. Sarah shot Jenny a glare but laid back and calmed down.

"Ok go ahead," Jenny said to the police officer.

"I'm sorry to say but we think that the two men that broke into your home and attack Mr. Moretti also attacked them and I'm sorry to say but they have passed."

Sarah broke down. *Why? Why? Why is this happening?* Jenny consoled her friend, she too wept for the Wilsons. The officer excused himself from the room. Sarah got herself composed again.

"Jenny, promise me that no one finds out that I'm pregnant. I am still pregnant, right?"

"Yes, you are and I promise."

"Does Frank or Sophia know?"

"No."

"Good. I don't know what is going on, but nothing more will happen, not to me, this baby, you, and no one. You're going to be an aunt. I can do this."

"We will do this. Don't worry you are not going to be alone. No one will know about the baby." Jenny swore to Sarah that day that this baby would be their secret. Sarah knew one thing; she wasn't going to let anything happen to the only piece of Luke she had left. She would protect her baby at any cost.

Even with all that has happened and as tired as Sarah was, she felt restless lying in the hospital bed. It was getting late and the nurse had just finished checking her for the night and shut her door blocking the noise coming from the hallway. Sarah normally wouldn't have minded but she hated not knowing what was going on. She wanted to talk to Sophia and Frank about what had happened and who the two men were but after Jenny had asked them to step out of the room to talk to her privately, they never came back. She thought that was a little odd considering all that happened. Sarah was so confused by everything and how no one seemed to want to clarify what happened. She even tried calling Sophia and Frank but neither answered nor called her back.

She sighed heavily and grabbed the remote for the TV. She had always been able to go to sleep to the TV. and hoped that it would work this night. She had just caught the ending of one of her favorite movies and although she had seen it a million times she was irritated that she missed it now.

"Breaking news, next at 11:00, stay tuned," the news anchor woman said. That caught Sarah's attention. She looked at her cell phone and checked the time, a couple of minutes before 11. She was hoping it would be something that would be interesting enough to distract her from her thoughts.

"Good evening to all of you just tuning in. Melanie is standing by with an update on the weather but first breaking news in our own backyard; we will go to Peter who is standing by on location, Peter what's going on?"

"Well Kara this street behind me, according to the ones that live here, is a sleepy street, nothing ever happens here one neighbor said, but that all changed a few nights ago. Now police won't let us go down to the houses involved nor tell us too much other then that two men kicked in a door to one house and attacked two women and the owner of the house next to the women came to their aid and in the struggle was stabbed. The two men managed to flee the scene and are currently at large. I found out that the injured man had under gone surgery and was listed as critical.

"Oh my! Do the police have any leads on the two that got away Peter?" the news anchor asked. Sarah laid frozen in place with her mouth dropped open in shock, her heart started to race and tears started filling her eyes.

"All they are saying now is that they have sketches of the men," the reporter paused.

"Peter is everything ok?" the anchor asked.

"I'm sorry, I'm just getting word that the

injured man was listed as being in a coma after the surgery, and apparently has gone missing from the hospital. The hospital has been under lock down. Here are the sketches of the men, please do not approach if you see them, just call the police and let them do their jobs. They are considered armed and extremely dangerous. The third picture is of the missing victim, if anyone sees these men call 911 immediately. Peter Smith reporting, Kris back to you."

"Wow, that's unreal, like a movie. Peter was this something that was random or did the victims know the intruders?" the anchor asked.

"Well from what we understand is that the women didn't know the men but that the neighbor that came to their aid did. Police are speculating it was a mistaken address and they are not saying anything more then that at this time. I will keep you posted if any new information comes to light," Peter said.

"Thank you Peter, unbelievable story, our thoughts go out to those victims and their families. When we come back a check of the 5 day weather ..." the news anchor was saying but Sarah tuned out her voice and the anchor's face was blurred through the tears. Seeing the sketches of the men and of Luke brought back that night into Sarah's thoughts. She laid there sobbing uncontrollably. She was growing tired of not knowing what was happening and realized that nobody was going to tell her in her current condition. Here she thought her life was confusing enough to find out she was pregnant with a man's baby she knew nothing about other then that he creeped her out and when she finally got enough nerve to get close to him she felt this incomprehensible pull towards him and it freaked her out and now he is gone. She was a mess and wondered if she was on the brink of having a break down.

"No, no I can't, this baby needs me and I need this baby," she said to herself. Just then the alarms on the monitors went off sending Sarah into a panic. A nurse came running in and studied the monitor, shut off the alarm and turned to Sarah.

"You need to relax. Your blood pressure just shot up," the nurse said in a low controlled voice and noticed that Sarah had been crying.

"What's the matter? Are you hurting anywhere?" the nurse asked with concern.

"Just saw the news," Sarah said softly as she wiped away the tears.

"Oh, that, well no more of that," the nurse said as she took the controller and put it in her pocket.

"Wait, what are you doing?" Sarah asked with disgust, "What if I want to watch TV?

"Just buzz us and someone will come in and turn it on for you. We need for you to relax and get that baby out of distress. That's our only concern, not you missing a TV. program."

Sarah knew the nurse was right and let out a big sigh, "your right, I'm sorry. Just restless and hate not knowing anything."

"I understand but you need to worry only

about you and your baby's health; nothing else. You don't want anything bad to happen do you?"

"No," Sarah whispered. She felt horrible.

"Ok. If you would like I could bring in some magazines, books, puzzles, something like that," the nurse finished.

"Thank you that would be nice," Sarah spoke softly and with that the nurse smiled and walked out shutting the door behind her. Sarah wanted to pull out the IV and leave the hospital but she had to think about the little one. She was so frustrated. She laid there watching the numbers fluctuating on the monitor until she fell asleep. ….

It was a dark, poorly lit, drafty room with stone walls. Sarah was lying on a cold hard ground with only a thin blanket covering her. She was freezing. She jolted up into a sitting position. *Where am I,* she wondered as she stood up looking around. Her heart started racing. No windows, the room had a musty smell and broken old thick metal rings that came out of the wall. She didn't want to know what those were used for. The room gave her the chills. Fear washed over her. She was cold and scared. She wrapped the blanket around herself and continued to look around the small stone room. There was a door so she walked over to it and tried to open it but it wouldn't open. It was locked. She started to pound on the door.

"Hello?" she yelled; nothing but the sounds of water dripping. She pounded again.

"Hello?" she yelled again and again

nothing. Her eyes started filling with tears. *Where am I*, she said to herself again as she turned and started walking away from the door.

The dim lights went out and it made Sarah jump and just as she was about to scream someone grabbed her from behind and covered her mouth. She tried to scream anyway but it was muffled. It was so dark; she couldn't see anything around her, not even to make out who had grabbed her. Her heart was pounding so hard she thought for sure it was sending her baby into distress. She struggled to get away but whoever had her was very strong and only held her tighter. She couldn't breath. As she started to cry she wondered what was going on. *Who has me, am I going to die?* The voice was screaming in her head. She tried screaming again but the hand only clamped harder over her mouth.

"STOP! Or I'll kill you now!" the deep raspy voice growled. That scared Sarah stiff.

Sarah gasped awake. Her heart was racing and she quickly looked around. She took a few deep breaths when she realized she was in the hospital and it was only a bad dream, but she lay there as still as she could be and quietly wept. The night drug on and Sarah tossed and turned. It never failed, as soon as she would get to sleep a nurse would come in and check on her and wake her back up. She couldn't wait to get out of the hospital.

Chapter 17

After Sarah insisted repeatedly that she was fine, and against her better judgment, Jenny left Sarah alone in the hospital room and went home to Robert. Sarah put up a good front even smiling on cue. Jenny hadn't left her alone much; Sarah thought it was in fear that she might do something stupid or crazy. But Sarah really wanted some time alone to process everything that had happened in hopes to answer some of her questions herself. Her thoughts were all over the place. She looked at her arm and followed the IV tubing up to the bag and let out a sigh. She hated hospitals. She wanted so badly to get up and go see for herself if Luke was really missing. She knew he was otherwise the hospital wouldn't be on lock down and there wouldn't be a police man posted outside her door. Just then the door opened and in walked a nurse holding what Sarah assumed to be her chart.

"How are you doing Sarah?" the nurse asked while looking at the monitor.

"Fine," Sarah responded with indifference.

"Ok just remember to stay calm, The Baby's heart rate is stable, so lets work on keeping it that way," the nurse instructed.

"Ok," Sarah responded with teary eyes. She was very emotional now and she hated that. The nurse saw it too and had an ideal.

"Would you like to hear the baby's heartbeat?" the nurse asked.

"Really? Yes, I would love that!" Sarah said excitedly.

"Ok, it will sound like a fast beat with a woosh,woosh sound," the nurse said as she reached over and turned a knob on the monitor.

There it was the most beautiful sound she had ever heard and hearing it was very comforting. Sarah ran her hands over her stomach and smiled.

"I hear you little one," she whispered at her belly. The nurse started to turn it off.

"Wait, please could it be left on?" Sarah asked.

"Sure," the nurse said seeing how calm it made Sarah. She quietly walked out.

Hearing the heartbeat of her baby was so relaxing but it didn't slow down her inner voice. She wondered what Damien and Salvator had done with Luke. She knew deep down they had him. She so desperately wanted to know everything but knew it would be some time before anyone would tell her. She was now deemed fragile. A fragile condition, she heard a nurse say to Jenny. The officer posted outside her door gave her little comfort knowing that if Damien wanted to get to her, that he didn't need a door to do it. She couldn't believe that the whole warlock and witches thing was true. She always believed they were just myths. It was hard to wrap her head around that logic but knew if she said anything to anyone that she would be seeing a shrink. *If what Luke had said was true then why hasn't he come to me at night like he had done so many times before?*

What was this connection they had? He had felt it too. She felt stupid for leaving him that day the way she had. He didn't want her to go and now she will kick herself every day with wondering what would have happened had she stayed that day. At first when the men had kicked in her door she thought it was just a horrible mistake but when Luke had shown up he had call them by name and that Damien seemed to have known what he was doing that it was her he wanted to hurt. Sarah ached inside; she wanted more time with Luke.

As she sat there listening to the sweet sound of her baby's heartbeat she realized that she wouldn't be able to go back to her house. It wasn't home anymore. She couldn't stand the thought of being in a place where she would have to relive that horrible night over and over again. *How would I be able to move on or raise a child in that house? What if those two men came back? No, I can't take that chance*, she thought as she picked up her cell phone.

"Hello?" a deep voice asked.

"Hi Robert. It's Sarah."

"Hey you. How are you doing?"

"Ok I guess."

"I'll get Jenny," Robert said.

"No wait. I actually called to talk to you."

"Really? What's up?" that surprised Robert. Sarah had never called to talk to him before. It caught him off guard.

"I was wondering if that offer was still open about staying in the apartment above the garage."

"Yes it is. I don't think Jenny would have it any other way," Robert said matter of fact.

"Ok. I was also wondering if you could call your realtor friend and see if he would come here and meet with me. I want to put my house up for sale. I don't think I could ever go back there."

"Are you sure? Although, I think that's a really good idea and I was telling Jenny that I think we would feel better knowing you were here. You would have security and Jenny right here and you're going to need help once the baby comes."

"Yes, that I know, you don't need to sale me on the idea. I agree."

Robert laughed, "If it was only that easy with everything. That snide remark made Sarah laugh to. She knew what he meant.

"Ok, then its settled. I will contact him first thing in the morning and Jenny will be thrilled when I tell her, or did you want to talk to her?"

"You go ahead. I have taken enough of your time. Sure you're ok with all of this?" Sarah asked not wanting to impose.

"Absolutely, I knew when I married Jenny that you were apart of the package," Robert said laughing. Sarah couldn't help but laugh at that.

"Ok, thank you so much for helping. I appreciate it," Sarah said.

"Your welcome, now get some rest, ok?"

"Ok," Sarah said softly. They said their good nights and hung up.

Sarah felt relieved. She decided that she would put everything behind her for the sake of her sanity and for the baby. She knew it wouldn't be easy seen is how Luke was constantly on her mind but she needed to think about the baby now. She couldn't sulk on what might have been or could have been. She couldn't fathom that Damien wanted to hurt her, someone he had never met before. She did vow that she would find out what happened and why, but for now she wasn't stable enough and she didn't want anything happening to the baby. She didn't want to lose her baby. Even if it killed her from boredom she decided that she wouldn't do anything but lay in the bed and focus on the sounds of her baby's heartbeat. She wanted to get out of the hospital sooner then later.

The nurse came in to check on her and saw that Sarah was still listening to the baby's heartbeat. Whatever made her relax was ok the nurse had told her. That made Sarah smile. The nurse had also brought in some magazines, puzzle books and books to help Sarah pass the time.

"You know if you stay calm and do what the doctor instructed, I can see you leaving within a week," the nurse said.

"A week?" Sarah screeched.

"Better then the alternative don't you think?"

"Yeah," Sarah huffed with a heaviness to her voice.

"I know it's not ideal but you have been through a lot and you were very dehydrated. We just don't want you going home to soon and have to come back," the nurse tried to talk sense into Sarah.

"I understand and I will do my best to be a model patient from here on out."

"Ok good, that's what I like to hear," the nurse said with a smile, "your dinner will be here shortly."

"Ok," Sarah said as she picked up a magazine and started reading it.

Finally, after almost a week and a half later, Sarah was leaving the hospital. Jenny and Robert came and got her and brought her back to their house. Although she was thankful for them, she knew her life would never be the same. The ride to their house seemed to take forever. It was raining, *perfect!* Sarah thought as she rested her head against the window and watched the rain hit the window and run down. She was in such a trance she hadn't realized that Jenny was watching her, worried. Robert put his hand over Jenny's to get her attention.

"She will be ok," Robert mouthed.

"Hope so," Jenny mouthed back as she looked down at their hands intertwined. She wished that Sarah could find what they had.

"Give it time," he said gently squeezing Jenny's hand. Jenny looked at Robert and gave him a loving smile. She thought that she was the luckiest woman alive to have a man like Robert.

They finally made it home and Sarah managed to drag herself up the stairs to the apartment that Robert and Jenny had fixed up for her. She couldn't wait to get back to some kind of normal life.

It was late but Sarah didn't want to go to sleep. She hated having nightmares and although she wasn't having the one of the dark shadow anymore, now knowing it was Luke and Damien, her new nightmares were just as equally disturbing. She turned on her laptop and decided to try and do some research. She goggled witches in Italy and returned nothing. She tried searching Luke, Damien and Salvator's names but still nothing. She added castles to the line and a number of hits came up. It was on the second page of the results when Sarah found what she was looking for. The castle she had seen in Italy. Damien's castle. She read the article. It was hundreds of years old and it was said to belong to a very evil man, legend said he was a warlock, a male witch. *Legend my foot*, Sarah hissed. The legend also stated that he had disappeared around the time of the witch hunts and trials and then resurfaced. Some people were supposedly reported as saying that he didn't make it through the witch hunts, that he was killed and its only his spirit haunting the castle. It was also said that he was being sought after by authorities in the deaths of a few people but that there was no real evidence to prove such a claim. *Now there is,* Sarah said to herself, *and yet he still manages to get away.*

She wrote down references the articles listed and looked them up. *Hmm, more books and articles, wonder if its all just hearsay and myths*, she said again to herself.

Sarah read a few more articles, basically all of them saying the same thing, no real account for anything. He was an evil, sneaky man.

The only relatively new news was the stuff involving her, and that even confused her. What did he want with me? Why did it involve Luke? She had wished she would have kept copies of the research from Italy but had turned them all over to her company for their file. But then again, she had no idea she would be wrapped up in the middle of all this mess. She wondered if Damien had a hand at blocking her in finding out her ancestors and the genealogist's disappearances. Her head was swimming with questions. She looked at the time and dialed Frank's number. She was getting tired of getting Frank's voicemail all the time but left him a message anyway.

"Frank it's Sarah again. I was hoping you would have some answers to questions I have. I need to know what happened and who Damien and Salvator are. Please call me back, Please!" Sarah paused then ended the call. She sat there staring at her cell phone, half wanting it to ring and knowing it wouldn't.

She didn't blame him really. He had tried calling when she was in the hospital but she didn't want to take anyone's calls. He must have taken that personal. Sarah tried a few more ways to look things up but to no help.

Sarah couldn't fight sleep anymore and knew it wasn't good for the baby so she turned in, praying to get a good nights sleep. She was pleasantly surprised to wake and find that it was 10 in the morning and she felt rested. It was a sunny day and decided to go for a walk. She went over to the house to see if Jenny wanted to go with her. Sarah knocked a number of times but no one answered. *Robert must be home*, she thought and headed out. She didn't get very far when her cell rang.

"Hello Frank!" Sarah said, glad that Frank finally got back to her.

"Hi Sarah, sorry it's taken so long to get back to you. After we got back here things got really crazy and then trying to get focused back on work. You understand," Frank said. Sarah heard a weird tone to Frank's voice.

"I suppose?" Sarah said with question, "Is everything alright Frank?"

"Ah, yes why do you ask?" Frank responded with a shaky voice.

"You sound different."

"Um, no. Just really busy."

"OK, well I was hoping you could answer the questions I have about what all took place," Sarah said careful to listen to Frank's tones.

"I suppose. Um, well I am coming to the states on business in a week or so. We could get together then and I will tell you what I know, but not by phone," Frank said. *His tone was really off.? Almost as if he was afraid to talk. What was going on over there* Sarah wondered as she agreed to meet Frank within the next week.

"But just so you know, I *DID* try to call you," Frank blurted out.

"I know, I had a lot going on, I'm sorry,"

"Don't worry about it. See you in a week," Frank said abruptly.

"Ok, bye," Sarah said as she heard him hang up. *How bizarre*, she thought. She looked down at her belly. *I'm glad I can still hide you*, she whispered and she continued on her walk. It felt good to get out in the fresh air.

Chapter 18

When Sarah was finished with the walk she stopped by jenny's house but still no answer. She went up to the apartment and looked at the calendar to see what she had planned the following week, nothing. She was back at work but only part time in her office and the other from home. Mr. Davis was easing her back into the work force. She was very thankful that he was understanding. The company was still the best one to work for and she was the first to point that out to anyone who would listen.

She went into her room and looked at herself in her full length mirror and pulled her shirt tight. *Hmmm, I think I can still get away with hiding you,* she said to her belly. She heard a knock at her door and figured it was Jenny.

"It's about time." Sarah said pulling the door open, "Oh sorry," Sarah said a little embarrassed, it was the mail man.

"I get that all the time," he said laughing

harder handing her a package.

"Thank you," Sarah said to him. He smiled and left.

Sarah looked at the package. It was from Sophia. How strange, she thought considering she wouldn't take her calls and she didn't think she told anyone where she was. She took the package into the kitchen and opened it. A letter sat on the top of the contents.

Dear Sarah,

I ran across this while going through some stuff and thought you would like them. Sorry for not calling but it's been real hard and I can only focus on my family right now, please forgive me.

Yours truly,
Sophia Moretti

Hmm, she mouthed as she put the note down on the counter and looked in the box. She pulled out what she figured to be a frame. She unwrapped it and sure enough it was, with a picture of Luke. She just stared at the picture studying every part of Luke's face. He was absolutely gorgeous. This picture was exactly what she needed. For the past few months she only had an image of him in her head but now staring at his picture, a flood of tears went running down her face. She held the picture against her chest as she looked in the box again. She reached in and pulled out a pouch this time. It looked familiar to her. She opened it up and a note fell out.

This was on the counter in his condo in Italy, thought you would like it.
Sophia

She had seen the pouch before but in the trunk in his closet. She emptied the contents into her hand. Just as she thought; the medallion. She put it on around her neck and looked in the mirror. It was so detailed. She wondered if it had some kind of meaning. Sarah didn't take it off. She like the idea of having something of his close to her. She took his picture and placed it on her nightstand table and laid down on her bed and just stared at it.

"There's you daddy baby," Sarah said as she rubbed her tummy. She couldn't wait to hold her baby. She laid there and cried herself to sleep.

"Sarah?" a familiar voice asked.

"Hmm?" Sarah asked.

"Don't go," the voice said.

"I won't," she whispered back.

Sarah's eyes popped open wide. She sat up quickly and looked around. Nothing, she looked at the photo of Luke.

"I wanted more time," she whispered.

A week later Sarah and Jenny made their way to their favorite restaurant and waited for Frank. Sarah had told him noon. She was finally going to get answers to questions that have been haunting her for months now. They took a seat at a table that had a perfect view of the door. They anxiously waited. Sarah could feel her heart starting to race and knew that she had to stay calm, for the baby. She took in a few deep breaths and calmed down.

"Are you alright?" Jenny asked.

"Yes, just a bit nervous."

"Me too," Jenny said as she patted Sarah's hand with hers.

Noon came and went, no Frank. Sarah and Jenny sat there quietly each watching the time without being obvious about it. At 12:30 Jenny finally spoke.

"I don't think he is coming," Jenny said softly.

"Let me call him real quick," Sarah said and dialed his number. She ended the call and put the phone away.

"What's up?" Jenny asked.

"The number is no longer in service." Sarah said sadly and got up and started walking towards the door. Jenny didn't move, sad for her friend. Sarah deserved a normal life and up until now it's been one thing after another. Jenny got up and joined Sarah outside. The drive back to the house was a quiet one. Sarah didn't feel like talking.

"You know Robert is going out of town again in a few months so I was thinking we should go somewhere, where we can relax and have a good time."

"Really?" Sarah asked surprised that Jenny would want to.

"Yes, I think it would be good for you. For us. A fresh new start if you will."

"Sounds perfect," Sarah said as a smile crept across her face.

When they got back they went into the house and looked at a map that Robert had. They settled on Virginia Beach when Robert came home. Sarah excused herself to the apartment.

She felt restless again and couldn't just sit in the empty apartment and she didn't want to bother Jenny and Robert so she decided to go over to the office and check in with Mr. Davis. It felt weird to be sitting behind the wheel of her car again. It seemed like forever since she last drove.

She made it to the office late in the afternoon, hoping most of her co-workers would be gone for the night and that was fine by her. The ones that were still there bombarded her with questions. Questions she didn't want to answer. Mr. Davis saw and pulled her into his office. He gave her an update on all the cases.

"You know, Sophia tried calling you here when you were still in the hospital, but when I asked if she wanted to leave a message she just hung up."

"That's odd, she hasn't returned any of my calls, nor picked up when I have called."

"Hmm, that is odd. So to change the subject, when are you coming back to work full time?"

"Well I would like to come back soon, I need   normalcy.

"I agree, sulking around wont help anything. It's time to put it all behind you." He said trying to sound positive but looking at her like she was about to break and that was her cue to leave.

"Ok well I'm going to stop by my office for a few minutes then head out." Sarah said as she started to get up and walk towards the office door.

"Sounds good, oh by the way, how's the baby doing?"

"What?" Sarah asked in shock. She never told anyone but Jenny and thought she had worn something that hid the bump well.

"Jenny told me that you were, don't worry I wont say anything to anyone and don't be mad at her. She just wanted me to know so I wouldn't over work you." Mr. Davis said with a smile.

"I see," Sarah said clearly irritated and walked out. She could hear him say something but she didn't care. She would deal with it later. She went into her office and sat down at her desk staring at the pile of messages. She glanced through them quickly, sighed and then put them back down. She leaned back in her chair and closed her eyes for a moment. She could hear the hustle and bustle of the workers left trying to wrap up their day. She would give anything to have that drive back. Hopefully when she returned full time she would. As Sarah left the building, co-workers would stop her and ask how she was and some even thought she had quit, which made her chuckle.

She got in her car and drove off. It wasn't until she had put it in park did she realize that she was in the driveway of her house. She managed to drive there without a second thought. It was like she was on auto pilot and that scared her. She couldn't remember the drive there. She sat staring at Luke's house. It looked more deserted then ever. She found herself walking over to it. She passed the for sale sign in her yard as she made her way to the front porch of his house. She was drawn to it. She tried peaking in the windows, straining her eyes to see through the little cracks in the curtains, nothing but darkness. Sarah walked around the house looking at every window and tried to look into the ones within reach but the blinds and curtains were drawn in all of them.

The grass was very long and she was sure the neighbors were not happy with what was just a dark house to it now being an eye sore. *Bad for resale on theirs,* she smirked with a chuckle. The only neighbors she could stand were the Wilsons. She thought everyone else was pretentious.

She looked across the street at the Wilson's house when she came around to the front of Luke's house. The 'for sale sign' in their front lawn had a sold sticker across it. *Wow that was fast,* she thought and looked over at the one in her yard, and had a flash of that horrible night, seeing Luke laying there with blood all over, the lights of the ambulance as they followed behind it. She shut her eyes and hung her head for a moment to get composure. *I can do this*, she said to herself over and over.

Sarah opened the front door letting the sunlight filter in to the living room. She walked into the room and walked over to where she last saw Luke. The night replayed in her head. She started crying. She took a deep breath in and went upstairs to her room. She opened the door and froze. Her room had been ransacked.

"What in the hell?" She said out loud. She walked in cautiously and took a look around; it didn't appear that anything was missing. A noise came from behind her and she jumped. Her heart started racing and Sarah whipped around and stared down the hall. Nothing was there. She slowly walked down the hall and stopped before the stairs to listen again. She could hear a faint noise from the spare room at the end of the hall. Her heart was racing and she didn't know if she should open the door or leave, but curiosity again got the better of her and she went to the door. With a shaky hand she opened it slowly. To her relief, the window was opened and a breeze had been blowing. She walked over to the window and looked out as she shut it. She could see her neighbors behind her house having a BBQ and clearly having fun. She envied that. She let out another sigh and went back to her room. She packed a few things in a gym bag and headed down stairs. She couldn't bare to look back into the living room so she just walked right out the door.

Sarah caught herself looking back in her

rear view mirror at the houses, hoping to see Luke's car pulling in or out, but no sign of him. *Of course.* Sarah made a stop at the store and then made her way back to the apartment. Jenny still wasn't home yet, which she was happy about. She wasn't feeling social. She unpacked her groceries and the gym bag, and then sat on her bed with her diary. She thumbed through it and realized that she wrote a lot about Luke. She read and cried until she again fell asleep.

Sarah returned back to work and in the first couple of weeks she had co-workers asking questions but after that the questioning had faded and it was work as usual, at least until her baby bump got bigger. The outfits that were able to hide the bump were getting tighter by the week. She would catch Mr. Davis staring at her stomach a few times and reminded him to not be so obvious about it. He would apologize and look away embarrassed by getting caught. This would make Sarah laugh knowing he would do it again. She thought that he was more excited then he let on.

Mr. Davis seemed to be very fond of Sarah. He had taken her under his wing and on many occasions told her that she was his best employee. Sarah was told once by Mrs. Davis at a company dinner that it was because she reminded him of their daughter, that she looked just like her, but that their daughter had been killed tragically by a drunk driver. *That explained a lot with how Mr. Davis acted with her,* she thought as she looked at him one day while in a meeting, *he probably see's his daughter in me and now this baby represents what it would have been like if his daughter would have been having the baby.* Anyone else would be creeped out by this but not Sarah. She actually found it comforting. She used him in a way too. She not only thought of him as a boss but as a father figure too. She valued his opinion as much as a daughter would a father.

A number of months had passed and Sarah was on the downhill slope of her pregnancy. She had to endure the whispering behind her back at work but she didn't pay any mind to it. She looked forward to the trip her and Jenny were about to go on. She was glad that they decided on Virginia Beach, they both loved the water and it was suppose to be really warm. They had gone to the beach during the summers when they were kids with Jenny's parents.

Robert ended up having a two week trip so they knew they didn't have to rush the trip. It had been a rough year and it would be a great way to unwind and rejuvenate. She was looking forward to the massages and facials that Jenny had booked for them.

The first few days at the beach were very relaxing. They walked the beach, got the massages and facials, tried new cuisines and slept in. She hadn't felt this at peace since Italy. They were lying on the beach, Jenny in the sun and Sarah under a big beach umbrella. Jenny was getting hot and wanted to take a dip in the water and Sarah declined to go, she was too relaxed so she just watched as her friend went into the water. Sarah was so relaxed, so warm that she ended up drifting off.....

She was walking up spiral stairs, the walls and ground were big stone blocks, it was cold and drafty and lit only by flickering candles.

She stayed against the wall as she went up, afraid of not knowing what was at the top. The place didn't look familiar but she seemed to know where to go. She got to the top and there was a long hallway in front of her, it was dark and creepy. She grabbed one of the candles from the iron candelabra hanging on the wall and started walking down the hallway, slowly, trying not to make noise with each step. As she walked she kept herself against the wall and kept looking back. She had a feeling that she was being watched, her heart was pounding. There were a lot of doors but it was as if she already knew which one to go to. Sarah's heart was racing so fast she couldn't catch her breath and she was scared but determined to get to that door.

She could see it up ahead only two more doors to go. She heard a noise behind her and she spun around, nothing was there, just darkness. *Where am I?* She wondered as she slowly turned back around and headed towards the door again. She put her hand on the door knob and a rush of sadness, pain and love flooded her body and she quickly let go. Tears began to stream down her cheeks. The need to open the door was too great. She put her hand back on the knob again but nothing. She turned it slowly creaking it open. She looked down the hall both ways; nothing. She looked in the room.

The room was dimly lit, but lighter then the stairs or the hall had been. She slowly walked in and looked around. It was a huge room. There was a huge four poster bed like the one she had in Italy and it had sheer drapes hanging from it. She was drawn to it. In a trance like state she walked over to it blocking out everything else around her. As she got closer she could make out a silhouette of a body lying in the bed. Her heart was racing but surprisingly to her, she wasn't afraid of whoever it was. Sarah reached out to pull back the curtain and just as she was about to see who was lying there, she was grabbed from behind, fear ripped through her, she tried to scream, struggling to break free but couldn't. She was drug back down the stairs and then down a dark hallway. She heard a door open and she was thrown inside a small room and as she landed she hit her head, losing consciousness. ......

"Sarah?"

"SARAH!?!"

"Hmm?" Sarah squinted as she came too. Jenny was standing over her.

"I think we need to get you out of the heat. You just scared the crap out of me," Jenny yelled in a panic.

Sarah agreed, she was still out of sorts. *Another weird dream*, she thought. She wanted to share them with Jenny but didn't want to alarm her, especially after what they had gone through.

She needed to move on but found it hard when those dreams wouldn't end. Jenny helped Sarah up and they made their way back to the hotel room. Sarah was exhausted but didn't want to fall back to sleep but couldn't keep her eyes open.

Chapter 19

By the time Sarah realized it, their vacation was over and they were heading home. She spent most of the time looking out the window while Jenny was on the phone with Robert. She was glad to be going home. She looked over at Jenny and watched her as she talked to Robert. Jenny was beaming. Sarah could see the love Jenny felt for Robert, she envied that, she ached for that but she was very happy for Jenny. She hoped that Jenny will hold on to that feeling for the rest of her life.

Finally after a long drive, they pulled into the driveway. They sat there a moment and thought of their trip and both agreed it was good. Cleansing if you will, Jenny had said. That made Sarah smile. Jenny went into her house and Sarah to the apartment. She put her suitcase down by the washer and threw her coat and purse on the table as she walked by it towards the bedroom and got undressed. Sarah went into the bathroom and ran herself a bath. She laid there with her hands on her stomach that stuck up past the bubbles. She was amazed at how big her stomach had stretched. The baby kicked and it made her hands move.

"Awww, hello baby Max or Maxine," she said as she poked at her belly. She never wanted to know the sex of the baby. The pregnancy was a surprise so it was only fitting the sex would be too.

She was getting a kick playing with her baby through her tummy. She would poke or push and the baby would push back. In that moment nothing else mattered, only the time she was having with the baby. The water started turning cold and she was getting tired so she decided to get out. She made sure everything was locked and crawled into bed. She was exhausted, as she was most of the time these days. She fell right to sleep.

"Where are you?" the voice asked softly.

"Right here. Can't you see me?"

"Put your hands out," the voice instructed.

"Why?" Sarah asked confused.

"Put them out," the voice instructed again softly.

"They are," Sarah answered.

"I can't find you," the voice said sounding further away.

"Hello?" Sarah called out.

"I can't see you," the voice spoke again even fainter then before, "Don't go."

"I'm here" Sarah yelled out.

Nothing.

"I'm here," Sarah yelled out again.

Nothing again.

Sarah woke up to see daylight coming from behind the blinds. She stretched and then laid there thinking about her dream. *What do all these dreams mean?* She wondered. She slowly got up, taking a little longer trying to move around her belly. She found herself pretty comical. She managed to get herself ready and went off to work her half day schedule.

She settled in behind her desk and started looking at old files that had built up. For the most part the cases were fairly easy to get through, typical research, *boring actually*, she sighed. She wondered if Mr. Davis gave her these simple cases to keep her work load down and no brainers because of her getting close to the end of her pregnancy. Any other time she would have gone to Mr. Davis and asked what was up but at this point she didn't care. Her mind was else where as she looked down at her growing belly. She was done with the small pile of cases and decided she had better look through the pile of messages. Only one caught her attention. It was from Sophia. Sarah was confused by it only because the date and time her secretary had put down. It was about the same time she was trying to call her but she would never answer nor call her back. Why would Sophia call here but leave no message. She picked up the phone and dialed her number.

"Hello," a familiar soft shaky voice said. It was Sophia.

"Hello, its Sarah."

"Oh, um, hi, what can I do for you?" Sophia said as if she didn't want someone to know who she was talking too. Sarah found her behavior odd to say the least.

"Ok, I'll bite. I have been trying to call you and then I get a message here at work that you had called. What's going on? And what's going on with Frank. He stood me up a while back and now his phone isn't in service. Why are you all acting so weird?" Sarah rattled on trying to get it all out before she was interrupted.

"Frank was in an accident. Anyone you seem to be around ends up hurt. I can't talk to you anymore."

"Hey wait that's not fair. You hired me to do research for you, and those two men were connected to your family so don't put that on me. You know, never mind, I shouldn't have called. Good bye." Sarah said and quickly hung up. She was mad that Sophia talked to her like that. She took a deep breath and realized what Sophia said. Frank was in an accident. *Oh god.*

She typed in Frank's name in the google line of her computer and hit send. She went through the results and there it was; a link to the news story. She clicked on it and read the little article that had come up. It didn't say much, just that there was an accident and that the authorities were investigating the suspicious circumstances behind the crash.

Sarah was frustrated. *Stay calm*, she told herself. She deleted the sites and turned off her computer. She decided to stop looking, stop trying to call Sophia, she was done. It was better that way. No one else would get hurt. She gathered her things and closed up her office for the day.

The next few weeks passed relatively smooth and uneventful. She was finding herself going to bed earlier in the evening. She was exhausted carrying the extra weight. She felt as big as a house. Jenny loved how she looked; Sarah wondered if Jenny was on drugs. It made Jenny laugh. Their bond grew tighter, if that was possible considering how tight they already were. She had asked Jenny and Robert to be the god parents and without hesitation they said yes.

Sarah felt restless and couldn't get to sleep, couldn't get comfortable enough to fall asleep. She tossed and turned in her bed then would get up and watch a little TV then back to bed. It was late into the night when she finally drifted off.

She was being wheeled down a dark hall in a wheelchair. She felt groggy. She tried to look around to figure out where she was. She had seen a hall like this before. This one was a little darker but at the far end she could see light. She tried to talk but couldn't. She couldn't turn around to see who was pushing her. She was too weak. *What's wrong with me?* She asked herself. The hall got lighter and lighter the closer to the room she came. The hall was big stone bricks, *have I been here before? This looks so familiar.* The light was starting to hurt her eyes. She was squinting to see but it was way to bright. It was making her eyes water, she had to close them.

"You're awake," a deep raspy voice said. The voice sent chills throughout her. She didn't know why but the voice scared her.

"Well you have made quite a mess out of something that should have been easy to take care of. I had to take care of it myself and for that you must pay. You will suffer like the ones before you," the voice said with an angry tone.

Sarah didn't understand what the voice meant, she was confused. She couldn't open her eyes, she was scared, and the voice sent chills through her body. She was trying to talk but nothing came out. *Suffer?* She didn't like the sounds of that. She hated not being able to see what was going on. Then, it didn't matter, the pain was excruciating. *OH MY GOD! Stop no! pleasssseee stop, oh god the baby.. No, no, please,* she was screaming but nothing was coming out. Someone was stabbing her in the stomach. The pain was unbearable.

Her eyes opened wide and she let out a scream. She looked around. She was in her bed, in a lot of pain. She looked down at her belly and then doubled over in pain. She screamed in pain again. She tried to reach for her cell phone on the night stand but the pain hit again and she curled up in a fetal position.

"Hee hee hoo, Hee Hee hoo." Sarah reached for her phone again. *Got it.* With shaky hands she dialed Jenny's number.

"Hello Sarah," Jenny said happily.

"Baby oooouuuuuuwwwwwhhhh," is all that came out of Sarah's mouth.

"I'M COMING! HOLD ON!" Jenny yelled in joy as she hung up the phone. Sarah could hear Jenny running up the stairs to the apartment. She must have used her key.

"Sarah?" Jenny yelled.

"In here!" Sarah yelled back through screams of agony.

"Ok ok. It's going to be ok," Jenny said as she entered the room to find Sarah doubled over. Jenny put slippers and a robe on Sarah and grabbed her hospital bag and helped Sarah down to the car. It took a few minutes to get down the stairs with Sarah having to stop to double over in pain at each contraction. Jenny and Sarah were in unison with the Lamaze breathing technique the Lamaze class had taught them. *They had to be quite the sight getting to the car*, Jenny thought as she giggled. Sarah shot her a mean look which made Jenny laugh.

Jenny helped Sarah get buckled in and off she sped towards the hospital. *She is one lucky person, the only one I know that could speed through town and never get pulled over*, Sarah told herself as she held on for dear life. They got there in no time. Jenny parked right outside the doors and ran inside, when she returned, she had a nurse pushing a wheelchair towards her. Once in the chair the nurse pushed Sarah quickly to a room and pulled a gown out of the closet. The nurse and Jenny helped Sarah get into the gown and settled into the bed. Everything was happening so fast that Sarah couldn't think straight.

Before she knew it, she had a belt around her to monitor hers and her baby's heart rates, an IV in one hand and her legs up and Jenny on her side telling her to push. The pain was nothing like she had felt before. Her lower body felt like it was on fire and she was being ripped into two. She was crying but as Jenny pushed her forward she found strength deep within to push. She was so tired but the doctor, nurses and Jenny kept telling her to push.

"I can't," Sarah yelled out.

"Yes, you can. Come on Sarah push," Jenny said loudly back to her.

"uuuuugggghhh," Sarah yelled as she leaned forward to push again.

"I see the head coming," the doctor said as a nurse handed him a mirror. "Look Sarah."

Sarah looked forward and saw the top of the baby's head peaking through. *OH MY GOD*, she breathed crying.

"Come on Sarah," Jenny barked.

"Sarah listen to me, on the next contraction I want you to push with all your might until the contraction passes. Don't stop pushing until then" the doctor instructed. The pain started, Sarah pushed.

"Push, push, push, push," the doctor continued to say over and over, Sarah pushed even though she felt like she was going to pass out.

"Stop pushing. The baby's head is out," the doctor said. Sarah was getting upset. *Push, don't push, make up your mind*, she thought as she glared at him. More pain.

"Push Sarah. A big push," the doctor instructed as Jenny helped lean Sarah forward to push. Sarah was exhausted. Then she heard the sweetest sound ever, the baby's cry.

"IT'S A BOY!" the doctor yelled smiling big while holding up the baby for Sarah to see. Sarah started crying tears of joy.

"You did good!" Jenny sobbed holding Sarah's hand.

After the nurses cleaned the baby, they wrapped him up and brought him over to Sarah and laid him on Sarah's chest. Sarah immediately wrapped her arms around him and pulled him in close.

"Hi there Max," Sarah said softly to her son.

"He is the most beautiful baby I have ever seen. He is perfect." Jenny said through her tears.

"Yes he is," Sarah agreeing.

She couldn't take her eyes off of Max. Then it hit her. He was a part of Luke too. She wondered if he would be like his father. *Would he have the abilities of his father in him? Guess we will cross that bridge when we got there.* But for now, all she cared about was the precious baby in her arms. Nothing else mattered.

After a bit the nurses had to take him to run the normal blood work and tests on him. Jenny told Sarah she would go with them to watch over Max. Sarah was thankful Jenny was there. The nurse told her that it would take some time that it would be good for Sarah to squeeze in a nap. Sarah didn't argue; she was so tired. Her eyes shut quickly.

"Come to me," the soft voice whispered.

"I'm here," Sarah whispered back

"Not close enough," the soft voice said.

"I'm trying," Sarah replied.

"Not hard enough. I want you."

"Want me?" Sarah said puzzled.

"Yes."

"I'm here."

"I can't feel you," the voice now faint.

"I can barely hear you," Sarah continued to whisper.

"Hello?" Sarah asked.

Sarah's eyes opened. The door to her

hospital room opened and Jenny walked in with baby Max in her arms and a nurse in tow. It took a minute for Sarah to come out of her sleep all the way. She knew that voice. She wished he was here. She sat up and got comfortable, and then Jenny placed Max in her arms. He felt so good there. She leaned her head down and kissed his forehead. She left her lips against his skin and took in a breath. He smelt so good. She didn't think she could ever let him go.

Epilogue

Sarah stood at the end of her driveway staring at her house like she had the day she bought it. She remembered that day. How excited she was to be buying her first house and how accomplished she had felt, she now looks at it with very different eyes. Her eyes filled with tears and as she tried to shrug off the sadness her gaze fell on the dark house next to hers. Tears ran down her cheeks. She missed his touch. She wondered everyday what it would have been like. The grass was over grown in that yard. It was obvious that he was no longer there and no one was looking after it. The curtains were drawn in every window.

I shouldn't have come here, she thought as she turned around and looked across the street at the house that use to be the Wilsons. She hadn't been back to this place since that horrible night nine months ago, other then that brief visit. But with her house sold, she had to say goodbye. Goodbye to that part of her life and she had to be sure that there was no signs of him being at his house.

"Sarah, we need to get going," Jenny said out the window of her car. "It's your birthday and Halloween after all, if we don't get moving now we will hit traffic and I don't think this sweet little boy of yours will be too happy about that," Jenny said knowing baby Max's feeding schedule better then Sarah. Sarah was extremely thankful for Robert and Jenny. They took care of getting all her belongings out of the house and getting set up with a realtor to get the house sold and for putting her up in the apartment. Yes, she was very grateful to have them in her and now Max's lives. She couldn't have picked better godparents for her son.

"Ok Jen," She looked one more time at the house that she had once called home, let out a big sigh, "goodbye," she said softly and got in the car.

"Are you ok?" Jenny asked as she glanced in the backseat at the baby and then put the car into drive looking back at Sarah.

"Yeah, I will be. It's hard to be here. I'm ready to put this behind me." Sarah said wiping the tears off her cheeks and watching as her old house and Luke's house faded away behind them as they drove off.

The Curse Chronicles
Dangerous Endeavors
Book II

Coming fall of 2012

Becky's Wish
Now available on Amazon.com

.....This night would change Michael forever, sending his life spiraling out of control. The life he knew would no longer make sense. The career he was so passionate about would no longer mean anything to him and the support from his friends would no longer matter.

On his quest for death, while in a drunken stupor, he crosses paths with a 12 year old girl, who only has one wish. He had never met her before, nor would he ever, but because she inadvertently saves his life, he vows to do everything in his power to grant Becky's Wish.....

About the Author:

Maggie Kirk used a mix of life experiences and dreams to start her on her path to writing her first fiction novel Becky's Wish. She has three fiction novels in the works along with a series of children books. Readers can find her work on Amazon.com and on her website www.maggies-library.com. Maggie lives in Washington with her family.

Made in the USA
Charleston, SC
22 March 2012